So, it's a date. . . .

Halfway down the walk Connor turned back and blew me a little kiss that only I could see. Then he was gone, leaving me to float inside.

After Connor's visit, the house didn't seem quite as shabby as before. With a little paint, some killer food, and a great band, I could pull off the party here. I *would* pull off the party here.

Well, technically I had no choice. But that wasn't what I was thinking as I climbed up the stairs in a daze. I was thinking that if Connor Reese could ask me out, there was hope for any and everything.

Look for all the books in

#1 Julia
#2 Lucy
#3 Kari
#4 Trent

Available from HarperTrophy®
A Division of HarperCollins*Publishers*

Kari

Libba Bray

HarperTrophy®
A Division of HarperCollins*Publishers*

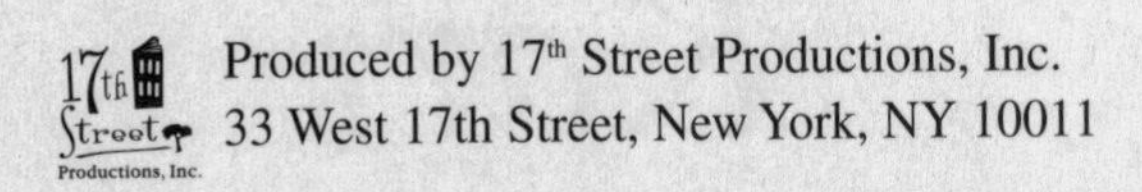

Produced by 17th Street Productions, Inc.
33 West 17th Street, New York, NY 10011

KARI

Library of Congress Catalog Card Number: 99-66680
ISBN 0-06-440817-5

To the three people who've made me braver:
Barry, Josh, and Charles.

And to Ann Brashares, for playing midwife.

chapter 1

There are all kinds of hell. Bowling. Getting your first period during sleep-away camp. Any Celine Dion song. My personal hell began unfolding as a Friday night trip with my younger brother and sister to the Couch Potato Video Emporium, "the finest collection of blockbuster hits in Greenway, South Carolina," to return what passed as family entertainment around my house. It was chore number three on my Friday night to-do list.

Couch Potato happened to be right next to one of the most happening spots in town, Café Vortex, a Zen coffee bar hangout where the hipsters and other beautiful people went to hear live music and just generally see and be seen. I'd personally never been there, not really fitting into that whole hip-beautiful-see-seen thing.

Since it was Friday night and every sixteen-year-old worth knowing was probably at a big Sweet Sixteen blowout, I figured no one would see me in my dateless state. Still, just to be sure, I parked the car in the middle of the nearly empty lot, far away from the action, and advised the sproutlings to sit tight if they knew what was good for them.

I dashed across the parking lot, keeping a firm grip on the humiliation fest of titles in my arms: *Vampire Go-Go Girls in Zombieland* (my sister's pick), *Stewardess Party III* (my brother's choice), *The Care and Feeding of Bats* (my grandmother, Lila), and *Steel Magnolias* (Mom). The plan was to slide the videos through the night drop box and walk away at warp speed. What was not in the plan was the videos getting stuck, which is exactly what happened.

With a big sigh I stuck my arm through the mouth of the Couch Potato Video Emporium, jamming my face up against the brick wall and sticking my butt out for balance. Not my most attractive moment. That's when I found myself staring into the most gorgeous pair of knees ever to grace a pair of khakis.

"Are you trying to rip off the place, or could you use some help?" The knees were connected to a voice. A mellow, coffee-rich voice with a hint of a drawl. The kind of voice that makes a girl forget she's left the house wearing a Looney Tunes scrunchie in her hair. I'd heard that voice once or twice in the halls at school and at least a thousand times in my daydreams. I'd just never heard it this close before. I peered up into the gray-green eyes of Connor I'm-So-Beautiful-It-Hurts Reese.

That face had played a starring role in my study hall fantasy for years. It was always the same fantasy with me as director: Open on wide shot of school commons. Zoom in as girl with larger-than-average brain and larger-than-average nose (that would be me) meets gorgeous boy with serious cool quotient (Connor). Lower boom mike as he says, "You know, I've been watching you for a whole year now. You're always in the commons, reading that same dog-eared copy of *Intro to Filmmaking*. Nobody could possibly be that dull. So I figure you have to be a genius feigning dullness to throw people off. Wanna rob banks together and raise a pack of wild genius children?" Cut. Print it. Roll credits.

Only in my head the script didn't include meeting my romantic destiny crouched in a potty-training position.

Connor was looking at me quizzically. "Seriously, do you need help?"

"Nope. I'm fine," I said. I went to stand up and toppled over, landing facedown on Connor's vintage 1940s wing tips. Even his feet smelled cool, like leather chairs and pipe tobacco and years of sun-drenched memories.

Connor reached down and picked me up under my arms. It tickled, and I couldn't help sort of giggling and snorting at the same time. It was an awful sound. This was the time in the spy movies when the hero started looking for his cyanide capsule. Unfortunately all I had on me were two crusty Midol and some dental floss.

"Thanks," I said in my best late-night DJ voice. I was trying to undo the giggling damage.

"Oh, hey. You dropped these." My family's horrible rentals were splayed out on the pavement for all to see. Before I could bust a move or take my life in dramatic fashion, Connor was picking up the plastic boxes and tucking them under his arm. "That drop box has been jammed for aeons. My advice? Let's drop these off with Norman Bates behind the counter inside."

He opened the door for me in the sort of gallant move that keeps a girl buying hair products. My mind was racing. What was Connor Reese doing at Couch Potato Video Emporium on a Friday night? Didn't he have a Sweet Sixteen party to attend? Or at least a marble statue to pose for? And how was I going to convince him that I wasn't the total bottom feeder of the high school food chain that I really was? I had to think. But how could a girl think standing next to such perfection?

The night crawler behind the cash register yawned, ruffling his three-day-old attempt at a goatee. "Those returns?" he asked.

"Yeah. Here," I said, trying to bury them under the boxes on his desk.

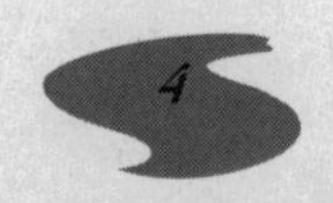

"Not so fast. I have to make sure you rewound them."

"Oh, they're rewound. The residents at the home are very conscientious about that," I heard my voice saying.

It's bad to lie, I know. But I was nervous, and sometimes when I'm nervous, my brain disconnects from my mouth and my mouth just *says* things.

"You rent videos for old people?" Norman Bates had found the energy to raise a slacker eyebrow.

Swallow. "It's a small thing, but it means so much to them. Look, I'll be right back. Maybe you should take care of . . . ah . . . er . . ." I was pointing at Connor.

"Connor Reese. At your service." He tipped his trademark fedora to me, revealing a head of close-cropped brown hair with bleached-blond tips and long sideburns. Cut to dream sequence of teenage girl running through fields of Connor Reese hair, stopping to kiss each babenificent follicle. Fade out on very happy ending.

"Thanks for the line cut," Connor said, sauntering up to the counter. I'm not being cute. The guy knew how to saunter.

I forced myself to walk away like I had something important to do. Safely hidden behind a stack of rentals, I peeked out at Mr. Gorgeous, straining to hear every syllable. Connor looked over and winked at me. I pretended to be extremely interested in the foreign film section. I debated how to begin our next conversation.

It's so great bumping into you like this. I've only been mooning over you since junior high. Do you suppose a popular guy and a girl who was raised by wolves could ever be an item?

Connor came up behind me. I instinctively picked up a random video box and pretended to read the cover. He peered over my shoulder. I could smell the Dial soap on him. I used Dial soap. It was a start.

He looked perplexed. "*Deux Petit Hommes*. Can't say I've seen it at the local megaplex."

"I . . . I've always . . . wanted to see it, actually. As an artistic exercise, of course."

Connor read from the back cover. " 'Two Siamese twin dwarves leave their provincial town and join the foreign legion in this uproarious French comedy from the director of *Les Bicycles*.' Uproarious French comedy. There are words you don't hear very often."

I quickly put the box back on the shelf. "Dwarves move me."

Fortunately he laughed. Another box caught his eye.

"*The Seven Samurai.* Somebody told me this is supposed to be good. Have you ever seen it?"

"No," I said. Honest answer. Another good start. "But I've read about it. It's a classic."

"You know a lot about movies."

"It's sort of a hobby of mine." Yeah, like breathing was a hobby of mine. Film was my life. I loved everything about it: the idea of crafting a story, shooting it, editing it just right. Art as total control. Not like life. "Actually," I said, straightening some out-of-order videos, "I'm applying to film school. To be a director."

"Whoa," Connor said, giving me a thumbs-up. "Planning to be the next Spielberg, are you? That's cool. I don't think I've ever met a girl who wanted to be a director before. I'll have to catch one of your movies sometime."

I could feel my face getting hot and knew it would be turning blotchy from a combo of pride, embarrassment, and devotion. Simultaneous emotions confuse my skin. I wanted to respond with something mysterious and femme fatale like, "Sometime ees not so ver-r-ry far away, *n'est-ce pas?*"

"So . . . were you ordering a video?" I said, settling for the indirect. Like I hadn't been dogging his every move.

He nodded. "*Ocean's Eleven*. Frank Sinatra. Sammy Davis. Dean Martin. Gotta love the Rat Pack."

"Definitely. Frank rules."

Connor and I walked outside into the night air, which seemed warmer and more alive than it had earlier. "You're Kari, right?"

"Kari Dobbins. Right." One hundred percent right. So right, you can't imagine.

"Most girls don't dig Frank. How'd you get so cool?"

"My dad. He was a fan." *Was*. I couldn't get used to saying that word.

"Oh," Connor said, aware that we'd entered a too-serious-to-go-there-on-a-first-meeting topic. He elbowed me in the ribs like guys do when they don't know how to change the subject. "So . . . you like Rat Pack movies, foreign dwarves, *and* suburban-mom tearjerkers starring Julia Roberts. Interesting. I wonder what else lurks behind the calm exterior of Miss Kari Dobbins, budding film director."

I was beyond mortified that he'd seen my family's rentals. But then he stuck his hands in his pockets and smiled that megawatt smile, and all I could think about was the movie starring me and Connor Reese. If I didn't take this opportunity to ask him out, I would kick myself. Years later I would bore my grandkids with the story about "the one who got away." With my heart beating wildly in my chest, I cleared my throat to speak. A girl's voice rang out, but it wasn't mine.

"There you are!" I turned around to see a moving Gap ad of sophomores, all fresh scrubbed and color co-ordinated, coming out of Café Vortex. There were three Gap girls, two Gap guys. I could do the math.

Nan Tatum's tinkly laughter floated on the breeze as she skipped up to Connor and threw her arms around him. "I missed you, baby," she purred. The sleeve of her pastel evening dress slid down, revealing a shoulder devoid of any blemish. It was the kind of shoulder men fought wars over. "What took you so long? I thought you said you were just checking on a video."

Connor took his hands from around Nan and let them hang at his sides. "I was. I did. Now I'm through."

"Good," Nan said, looking up at him through thick, dark lashes. She whispered the next part in his ear, but I heard it all. "You don't want me to be late to my own Sweet Sixteen, do you? I bet everybody's already there by now!"

Everybody but yours truly. So Nan Tatum was throwing the party of the season, and everybody who was anybody would be there. That would explain why I hadn't heard about it.

Deeper mortification began to set in. The whole time that I'd been blathering on like a complete dweeb in the video store, acting like I had even a chance with Connor, he had known he was on his way to Nan's big bash and that I was definitely not.

My stomach hurt at the thought. Could my life possibly get any worse? That, by the way, is a question you should never hurl out at the universe. The universe will answer big time.

Just then I was vaguely aware of a bleating sound in the distance, like a cross between a sick cow and a mariachi band. My brother, Theo, was leaning on our car horn.

"Yoooo-hoooo!" Theo called out in his best falsetto. "Time to make the doughnuts!"

Nan's best friend, Jen Appleton, flicked her long hair behind her shoulders and rolled her eyes. "Ex-*cuse* me . . ."

Theo leaned on the horn again and screamed as if he were being beheaded.

Connor gave me a sweet smile, which made me feel even worse. "I think someone's trying to get your attention," he said kindly.

"Foster kids," I deadpanned. "Troubled youth. We're hoping to rehabilitate them through video rental therapy. You know, *The Sound of Music*. *Rudy*. *Barney's*

Greatest Hits. That sort of thing." I made a mental note to torture Theo later by replacing his Korn CD with Britney Spears.

"Whatever . . . ," Jen said. "Nan, your mom will be majorly torqued if we're any later to your party. I can't wait to check out what the decorator did to the backyard. And Janice says DJ Dimitri is so unbelievable—"

"Jen . . ." Nan interrupted by glancing in my direction, then looking away. Jen followed her quick gaze to me and stopped midsentence.

"Oops."

"You know, I think some of my invitations didn't get out on time." Nan was speaking very slowly to me, like somehow being unpopular also made you partially deaf. "Did you get yours . . . Crystal?"

"Kari. I haven't checked my mail in a while. I'm out of the country a lot. Wow, look at the time. I better go. Happy birthday." I fumbled for my keys in my pocket, dropped them twice, then started walking in the opposite direction of the family car.

"Hey! Isn't that your car over there?" Jen called after me.

I shrugged and kept walking. "My car's over by the bookstore. Silver Honda." I clutched my keys so tightly, I could feel the imprint of them in my hand. Behind me I could feel Connor Reese disappearing from my life,

moving toward a future of glittering parties and Friday night football games.

I wondered how the scene would play if I rewrote it for a movie. Open on medium shot of heroine walking through empty parking lot. She wears a determined look and a stylin' new dress. Climbing into her shiny silver Honda, she stops to open a handwritten note left by a mysterious stranger in a fedora: You are invited to my amazingly swank life. Be there or else.

I waited behind OfficeMax till I saw Nan and gang soaring out toward town. Then I ran toward my real car and my soon-to-be-annihilated brother.

"You are so dead," I hissed at Theo as I threw open the driver's-side door of our family car, aka the Jesus mobile. The 1967 Dodge Falcon had been called that ever since one of my grandmother's more artistic boyfriends spray painted a replica of the Last Supper on the hood. Fortunately my grandmother—Lila, as she insisted we call her—dumped the artist for a vegetarian bullfighter before he could program the horn to play "Away in a Manger." Still, the car was a source of major humiliation for me.

"Let's get this show on the road. I have band practice at eight," Theo said through a mouthful of Taco Bell. He was playing Power Ranger of the radio—turning the dial so fast, we were treated to a postmodern playlist of static broken up by occasional bits of music. I reached over and turned off the radio. "Either play a whole song or leave it off."

Theo folded his arms across his chest. "Oooh, she gets her license and becomes a radio Nazi. This is how the corruption of power starts, folks."

"Shut up, Theo," I snapped.

"I don't remember taking a vote on keeping the radio off. Isis, do you remember taking a vote?"

"On. Off. In the final analysis, all is pain." Isis sighed and stretched out in the backseat, her long, black granny dress trailing in tattered spiderwebs over the cracked vinyl where the foam padding was coming out. She seemed much older than twelve.

"Are they teaching existentialism in sixth grade now?" I asked irritably. The car stalled, and I started it again, trying not to flood the engine, the way my dad had shown me years before. The engine stalled, then changed its mind and burped into action.

"Isis doesn't see you." Isis pulled her hand in front of her face. Faded henna markings crisscrossed her palm like a detailed road map to nowhere.

"What is this, goth *Sesame Street*? Stop referring to yourself in the third person, Rachel. It's so beyond annoying."

"The name is Isis now. Rachel no longer exists."

"Yeah, well, I miss her. And her normal wardrobe."

Theo grabbed at the wheel. "Could we get going, please? Tonight I'm laying down my rockin' clarinet part for 'White Rabbit' at band practice. This is the one that's gonna take us all the way to the top, ladies and germs." Theo rocked his head from side to side, moving his fingers in front of him in an air-clarinet solo.

Besides annoying me senseless and searching for signs of nonexistent hair growth on his upper lip, Theo's greatest passion was for Ina Godda Nagilah, the world's only acid klezmer band. As far as I knew, their only gig was the bar mitzvah of the drummer's cousin in Spartanburg. The cousin still blamed the band for his lousy money haul.

We pulled onto the access road, and I thought about my chances with Connor. Even though I'd made a complete fool of myself, even though he had a supermodel girlfriend, still I found myself hoping.

Just stop it, Kari, I ordered myself. I mean, it was time to face certain facts. Connor was dashing off to a glittering party in a BMW full of carefree popularity. I was stuck driving Vampirella and the Klezmer King around in a car that would have embarrassed even Elvis.

The Odd Dobbinses. That's what we were called around town.

It hadn't always been that way. As recently as four years ago, I could see isolated snapshots from a time we didn't talk about. My parents teaching Isis, the former Rachel Dobbins, how to ride a bike. Click. Mom wearing makeup and a starched white oxford shirt. I'm eating Goldfish and reading *Anne of Green Gables* behind her. Click. Theo all summer brown and freckly, running through the backyard sprinkler after Frisky when he was only a pup. Click.

And Daddy, looking serious by the BBQ grill, wearing a Because I'm the Chef, That's Why apron over the bad heart that would kill him three months later. So many times I'd looked at him and never seen the thing that mattered.

Click. Click. Click. But that was all before. Before we'd had to move into the Castle of Abnormality with my mom's mother, Lila, who raised iguanas and other creepy crawlies for fun. Before Theo had traded his boyish tan for fish-belly-white skin and a weird band. Before Mom had let her hair grow long and frizzy and started reading meaning into tea leaves and leftover spaghetti. Before Rachel became a gothster with a made-up name and the whole school started thinking of us as separate. Outsiders. Freaks.

Theo had been quiet for a whole thirty seconds. It was a stretch for him. "Okay, if you won't let me play

the radio, I guess I'll have to sing," he chirped. "Ready, campers? Kum-ba-yah, my Lord. Kum-ba-yah . . ."

Isis writhed in mock pain. "It burns! It burns!"

"Theo! Cut it out," I shouted. "Or I'll tell Mom." Okay, as threats go, it was just one step above "I know you are, but what am I," but I was driving. Plus it worked.

"You can't tell Mom. She's working tonight."

"Where?" I asked. Not that I really cared.

Isis piped up. "She's telling fortunes for some rich people over in Silver Shores."

I wasn't exactly loving my mom's fortune-telling business. It didn't help refute the alien Dobbins theory.

"Hey, Eyesore . . . ," Theo called out to Isis. It was a dance they did.

"Isis is not amused."

"Yeah, whatever. Listen, in a fair fight do you think Dracula could kick Batman's butt?" Theo proposed.

"Isis is not interested in having this conversation." She wasn't the only one.

"I mean, hypothetically. Batman has some cool gear. But then again, Dracula has that whole undead vibe going on."

Isis plopped her black-booted feet onto the headrest. The broken laces of her Dr. Martens tickled my neck. In the rearview mirror I could make out her Ministry sticker on the tongue of one boot, although it read YRTSINIM in the mirror.

"Do you mind?" I said, elbowing her foot.

Sighing, Isis sat up and dangled her arms over the front seat. "First of all, Batman is really playboy Bruce Wayne. He's still mortal. And—here's the crucial part—he's a comic book character. Dracula is based on a real fourteenth-century scaremonger named Vlad the Impaler."

"Ooh. Not a happy name at all. What do you think, Kari?"

"I think you should join a youth club. Maybe wear some decent clothes now and again," I suggested.

Isis snorted. "Lila says that's totally bourgeois thinking."

"Yeah, well, news flash—Lila is sixty-seven years old and insists that her own grandchildren refer to her as Lila so people will think she's still an ingenue. Her thinking isn't totally reality based. Are you with me, Rachel?"

"It's Isis. If you have any further questions for me, you can send them care of isis@realgoth.com."

"I'll be sure to do that," I scoffed. I started searching for signs of Nan's silver-blue BMW and totally missed my exit.

"Hang on," I said, streaking across a lane of traffic and onto the exit ramp.

At that very moment something scaly, damp, and long scampered across my foot.

"Ahhhhhhh!" I jammed my foot on the brake and screeched to a stop. I threw open the car door and leaped up on the hood just as the engine died. A large green lizard crawled out the open door and onto the busy road. It was Lila's pet iguana, George. What was he doing there?

"Somebody grab George!" I screamed. George logged on to my antireptile vibe and made a move toward me. I camped out on the hood, feeling the warm engine burning against my legs, possibly saving me from years of shaving duty.

The light was about to change. Two cars back, someone was laying on the horn like there was no tomorrow. Forgetting my temporary iguana phobia, I leaped over George and stormed past an irritated man in a Volvo.

"Hey, moron!" I shouted, then stopped dead in my tracks. It was Nan and the Gap kids. And Connor.

Connor yelled out, "Dobbins! What are you doing here?"

"My car stalled," I answered robotically. I couldn't let them see the car. I had to divert them somehow. "You're probably better off backing up and getting back on the Loop."

"Hel-*lo!*" Jen said. "We can't back up onto four lanes of traffic. We'll have to go around."

I was about to experience a drive-by humiliation. I stood completely transfixed as Nan pulled her gleaming Beamer even with the Jesus mobile. I willed the light to turn green, but it stayed as red as my cheeks.

"Nice Honda," Nan said with a laugh. "Who's that in the back? The Addams Family?"

In a flash Theo jumped onto the back of the convertible, brandishing George over his head in both hands. "I can't control him! He must feed, feed, *feed!*"

With a chorus of high-pitched screams and the screech of tires, Nan sped off, sending Theo and George tumbling into the bushes by the side of the road. A thick cloud of gray gravel dust floated over the spot where moments before, my evening had sunk to a new all-time low.

Five minutes later, with George secured in an old shoe box, we inched toward home. All I could think about was going upstairs to my room, kicking off my shoes, and sending in my application for the witness relocation program.

chapter 2

It was just past 8:30 P.M. when we drove up to our rambling, *Munsters*-style house. Lila had kept a torch burning for us. That's not a figure of speech. There was an actual tiki torch aglow on the front lawn. Its eerie light cast long, wavy shadows over the faces of Lila's fake Easter Island statues. Three carved wooden gods with great big bellies bloomed along our walkway like yard gnomes on steroids.

Our next-door neighbor had complained when Lila installed them during her primitive-art phase. Eventually he backed down. Everybody backed down when it came to Lila.

I was trudging up our front walk, wanting to be alone in my misery, when a blowtorch screamed to life a few feet away and made me nearly jump out of my skin. Lila held something over the torch, then snapped it off again.

"Didn't mean to startle you," my grandmother said without looking over at me.

"What are you doing?"

"Feeding Hefty." Hefty was one of her pet snakes.

She owned three. As a herpetologist, Lila had taught at the university and traveled the world, collecting interesting reptiles of all kinds. Long ago I'd learned to share my Cheerios with horned frogs and pull back my covers every night to check for unwanted visitors.

"You need a blowtorch to feed Hefty?"

"He likes things grilled, you know."

How I longed for one of those cuddly grandmas who bakes fudge and tells you your skirt is too short.

Lila marched toward me. In the light of the tiki torch her makeup looked harsher than usual. Bright orange lipstick circled her thin lips. She was wearing her favorite outfit—a lime green, psychedelic print polyester top with matching gaucho pants that she'd had since the sixties. If this outfit were an animal, you'd have to shoot it and put it out of its misery. Gray wisps of real hair stuck out from beneath her red pageboy wig. It was her date wig.

"Nice ensemble," I said. "Will you give it back to the wax museum when you're through?"

Lila pursed her lips playfully at me. "For your information, missy, I toured Madame Tussaud's with none other than the nephew of Winston Churchill when I visited London in '55. He was quite smitten with me." Hefty slithered across Lila's arm.

"Did anybody call?" I was waiting for a call from my best

bud, Jared. He was working on a new comic book and promised to give me a shout once he'd finished for the night.

"I don't bother with that machine. It's so bourgeois."

"I'm into bourgeois human contact with the outside world. You should try it sometime."

"You're very impertinent, did you know that? Hold on. Something came for you in the mail." Lila exhaled loudly and strode toward her gardening table, where a stack of mail was waiting, and handed me a large, official-looking manila envelope. In the darkness I had to strain to see the rubber-stamped return address: New York University.

I felt a little sizzle of excitement start in my feet. My college application was here at last. I made my way over the broken flagstones toward the front porch, cradling the precious envelope in my arms.

"Watch out for my arachnid project. It's on the porch!" Lila called after me.

Sure enough, a tarp was stretched across the paint-splattered front porch. Various dead spiders had been superglued to the tarp with their Latin classification names listed beneath them in calligraphy.

Lila fired up her blowtorch again. "It's going to look wonderful in the entrance hall, don't you think?"

For the billionth time I wished myself out of this carnival

of kooks and into a dorm room at NYU. I knew my family was "different," but I was different from my family, which made me the oddest Dobbins out. And the loneliest.

I opened the door and our mutts, Fric (formerly Frisky) and Frac, came tearing out, barking loudly. I could hear Lila cursing at them to stay back as I closed the door behind me. The house was in its usual disaster state. Books and magazines were stacked on every windowsill. The walls of our living room glowed with a sickly mustard color that my mother insisted was "warm Tuscan gold" when she painted it. It was more of a "sinus infection yellow."

The hallway by the stairs sported a large corkboard where Isis could post notes about her needs at the grocery store along with her particular philosophy of the day. Tonight it featured a large index card reading

- Tom's of Maine toothpaste
- Bugles
- Coppertone, SPF 45

If energy is neither created nor destroyed,
then why am I so tired all the time?

After discovering my answering machine behind the Cheerios box in the pantry, I dusted it off and hit the red button. Beep. *Theo, it's Eugene. Where are you? Band practice starts at eight. Not five after eight, man. We're professionals—* Theo's obnoxious fellow band geek. I hit erase. Beep. *Hey, Kar, it's me. Dee.* Real World *is a repeat. Major boredom. Did you know that even Sarah Bledsoe is having a Sweet Sixteen? I can't believe my birthday's in the summer when everybody's gone. I'm bummin'. Call me.* Beep. *Sweetie, it's Mom.* Party sounds nearly drowned her out. *Do me a favor? Collect Isis's grocery list and leave it on my nightstand? Thanks, honey.* Beep.

I took the stairs two at a time and undid the combination on my door. Then I flipped off my shoes and put on my old, worn slippers with the Daffy Duck heads on the front.

I needed mood music for such an important moment. Every good director has to know how to set the scene. Flipping through my alphabetized CD rack, I scanned over the *E*'s, *F*'s, and *G*'s till I hit the *H*'s and Lauryn Hill. Phat beats filled the room as I carefully slit open the envelope with my father's silver letter opener and pulled out my application to the nation's top film school.

Let the rest of the sophomore class scope each other out at party after party. While they were killing brain cells, I was getting the jump on my college education.

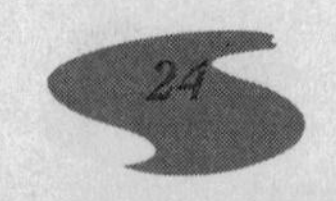

While they were playing tongue hockey, I was turning my passion for film into a career. While they were laughing and partying, I was . . . sitting on my bed. Alone.

No—bad thinking, bad! Bad!

I was planning every move in my glorious future! I was perfectly in control.

I spun out a little fantasy of myself accepting an Oscar for my first feature film, *Confessions of a Teenage Social Reject*. I'm wearing my borrowed Armani gown and half a million in jewels from Harry Winston. As I thank the people who helped me become the most successful female director in the history of cinema, Jen Appleton is watching from her trailer home with her ten children. Nan Tatum is sorry that she didn't invite me to her party and that she weighs over three hundred pounds because of an unfortunate gland problem. And Connor Reese is secretly cutting out pictures of me from *Vanity Fair* and wishing for what could have been.

The first two pages of the application were your basic 411—name, social security number, etc. It was the third page that got a little hairy.

At the top of the sheet were two sentences followed by a blank space: *Please list all extracurricular activities in which you have been involved, including clubs, organizations, charity work, internships, travels abroad, etc. Also list positions held, leadership roles assumed, awards and honors received, special projects hosted, and any other pertinent information that you would like to share with the acceptance committee. Note: The committee invites the submission of student films.*

I read it three times. It didn't get any better.

I was completely undistinguished. I'd been a member of the Spanish club for exactly one quarter. I'd sung with the Buccaneer Chorus till our choir director suggested I just mouth the words. And I didn't have a single film to submit. My hopes had just gone from zero to sixty and back to zero again in under two minutes.

The threat of a deep funk was looming. In need of a distraction, I punched number one on my speed dial.

A raspy voice answered after three rings. "Hi. I'm actually here right now, so if you want to leave a message, you'll have to call back after the sound of the tone."

"Skip it, Jared, it's me."

"Karnage. What, you mean you aren't donning the taffeta for Nan Tatum's Sweet Sixterror party?"

"Does everyone know about this party but me?" Great. Even Jared, the most antisocial person I know, had the download on the party of the century.

"Jen Appleton was blabbing her drill team mouth about it in study hall."

Okay. I felt a little better.

"I was just gonna watch *Duck Soup* on the nine o'clock movie. Wanna watch it together over the phone?"

"Can't. Gotta work on my application to NYU."

"Finally came, huh? Well, don't let me keep you. You've only got, what, sixteen months till the deadline."

"I'm a planner, okay? That's what separates the men from the . . . nonplanning men."

"Nice turn of phrase. Do I detect a cloud of tension in your Technicolor world?"

I slid off the bed till my scalp touched the floor. It was still my favorite position for major phone confessionals. Something about all that blood rushing to the head makes a girl say things. "It will take me more than sixteen months to make the list unless I can suddenly become an underprivileged Inuit with a mantel full of trophies and a heart murmur." My father's sweet, stern face watched me from a frame on my nightstand. I was instantly sorry I'd said that thing about the heart murmur.

"You lost me, Kar."

I read the dreaded passage to him.

"Whew." He whistled in appreciation. "These guys do not play around. So the Kar-meister is in desperate need of upping the social profile, eh? You'll think of something."

Was he crazy? I couldn't redeem myself in just over a

year. I'd have to become a whole new person. Lying there with my head on the floor and my heart in the basement, I felt irritated that Jared didn't understand how important this was to me. "It's going to take a miracle."

"Well, miracles happen every day. Besides, no one can cross the *i*'s and dot the *t*'s like you can. Or is that the other way around?"

"Thanks for your support," I growled.

"Look," Jared said, like it was painfully obvious. "They said you could submit a student film. So make one."

"You don't understand. I'd have to come up with an idea. Write a script. Rehearse some actors. Shoot it. Edit it. Correction—find some money and shoot and edit it. You can't just jump into making a movie."

"Sure you can. If you're not a complete control freak."

"I am not a control freak!"

"Of course not. Every sophomore updates a to-do list by the minute. Kar, you practically line up your shoes with a slide rule every night."

I glanced over at my partially open closet. A neat row of shoes smiled at me from inside. "Look. I just like things a certain way. That doesn't make me uptight."

"Whatever. Maybe you should take a few tips from Dee. She's got the laid-back vibe."

Dee was my best gal pal. She *was* good-natured, but

I hated being compared to anybody and found wanting. "Maybe you don't know Dee as well as you think you do." It was such a stupid, second-grade thing to say.

Jared, as usual, saw me and raised me. "Guess not. I saw Dee in the cafeteria the other day. She's really done that morphing thing girls do."

"What do you mean?" I asked, even though I knew what he meant. Dee had bloomed into a babe while I was still a babe-in-waiting.

"Just that she's . . . I don't know. Different these days. Maybe it's the hair."

And the body. And the face.

The sounds of Channel 11's nine o'clock movie theme crackled over the line. I was suddenly more tired than I ever remembered being. "I should go. Your movie's coming on."

"Another Friday night well spent. Before I forget, let's go to the mall tomorrow."

"What for?" I asked, yawning.

"I want to get my ear pierced."

This was news. "Why?"

"I'd tell you, but then I'd have to kill you."

Another Jared mystery. "Fine. But if you want to cut your hair into a rat tail, I'm drawing the line."

A note of irritation crept into Jared's voice. He was

getting more and more touchy and secretive around me. "What's wrong with getting an earring? Just last week you said guys with earrings were, what was the *Teen Beat* phrase you used? 'Hotties.' "

"Chill. We'll go. Pick me up at three, and don't be late." I let my legs tumble over my head and drop to the floor with a thud. My head still felt all tingly.

"Roger. Don't worry about the college apps. We'll get you in if we have to stage a musical benefit."

"Thanks, Jared." I sighed. I hit stop on my CD player and started hunting for Sarah McLachlan, my favorite pity party music.

"See you tomorrow," Jared said, then added, "and Kar?"

"Yeah?" I asked, hoping he had some last-minute words of encouragement. *You're too brilliant for NYU to ignore. You're so much cooler looking than Nan Tatum. You're nothing like your loser family.*

"Don't get all mopey about this and listen to Sarah McLachlan over and over, okay?" There was a click and silence. That's the trouble with best friends. They know you too well.

I know it sounds sort of pathetic, but as long as I was feeling like toe jam, I figured I might as well go for the total wallow. That's why I opened the closet door and found my father's old photographs. They were hidden

deep inside a shoe box I kept hidden on a shelf behind a collection of Barbie dolls missing various limbs. I was kind of hard on Barbie.

I opened the box and began sorting through the photos. I'd cataloged them according to mood and scene, like a good director would. There were family shots, vacation pictures, still lifes, and nature studies. I pulled out a still life first. Waxy fruit spilled out of a wooden bowl in front of a window. He'd gotten the light just right, so that the banana looked yellow and perfect. No bruises. No icky spots on the apples.

My dad could've been a top-notch photographer. Instead he'd spent his days working in an office, overseeing data entry clerks and stuffing his dreams down where no one could see them.

The phone rang downstairs, but I ignored it. I pulled out a picture of Mom from the family stack. She was seated in our old living room with the beige sofa. Isis was curled up in her lap. She couldn't have been more than three. Mom looked young and beautiful with a closed-mouth smile and red lipstick. Something about the photo unsettled me. Like there was something missing. And then the sadness crept up on me like a ghost. It was my favorite way of torturing myself, looking at Daddy's photos. Like if I looked hard enough, he'd show up in one of them and spring to life again.

Isis gave a quick knock and barged in my room. "Mom called. She needs you to pick her up from that party. And she said to bring your camera so you could get some airtime of her reading fortunes."

The last thing I wanted was to pick up my mom from some geriatric party in Silver Shores—or to get footage of her in action predicting life changes and maybe a toe bunion. "Can't Lila do it? I'm comfy."

Isis held out a piece of paper. "I'm just the messenger. Here's the address."

Reluctantly I grabbed the address: 1024 Stonington Lane. Deep in the heart of exclusive Silver Shores. I grabbed my keys and started to change, then thought better of it. Why should I care what a bunch of rich old geezers thought of me? In silent protest I kept my Daffy Duck slippers on, readjusted my scrunchie, and set off with my camera to record ten minutes of extreme boredom.

chapter 3

It took twenty minutes to cross town into North Greenway, Land of the Beautiful People. The headlights of the Jesus mobile threw a beam onto the cutoff for Silver Shores, A Luxury Community, as the sign said. No duh.

I drove far into the maze of mansions, each more beautiful than the last. Stonington Lane popped up on my right, and I followed it to 1024. A massive, newly built house with arched windows everywhere stared down at me from the top of a small, amazingly landscaped hill. From the car I could see people floating by those windows inside the well-lit house.

I closed my eyes for a minute and imagined what it must be like to live that way, with everything clean and neat and totally in place.

The front door opened a sliver, and a couple in formal wear ran out and around the back. Once they'd disappeared behind a tall hedge, I made my way up the hill with my trusted party cam strapped across my shoulder and rang the bell. Even the doorbell sounded happy to be there. Party sounds beat against the windows. Looking down at my feet, I wished I could rethink the shoe thing.

A woman about my mom's age answered the door. She had her blond hair pulled off her face in a gold clip and a tan courtesy of the Silver Shores Country Club. She gave me a wary smile. It looked familiar for some reason, but I couldn't think why.

"Hi. I'm Kari Dobbins?" I said. It came out as a question. "My mom is here. She asked me to come film her reading."

The woman opened the door wider. "Oh. You're the tarot card reader's daughter." That wasn't exactly how I wanted to be remembered for posterity. "Come on in. She's out back."

I stepped into a dream. The foyer was tall and open. A waiter whizzed past me, carrying a silver tray filled with yummy food things. Now this was a party straight out of the movies. Cut to our heroine, we'll call her Kari, in a long, flowing evening gown. She tap-dances into the party on the arm of her tuxedoed date. Camera pulls back on a wide shot. They glide. They twirl. They run hand in hand up to their hostess in white, who says, "So nice to meet you, Kari. I'm Mrs. Tatum."

Cut, cut, cut!

I stared at the woman. Tatum? As in Nan Tatum's mom? This couldn't be happening. The scene in the living room confirmed my worst fear. This wasn't some

old-timers club. This was Nan Tatum's Sweet Sixteen party! I was surrounded by the coolest cliques of Greenway High: the preppies, drill teamers, cheerleaders, jocks, do-gooders, and other assorted people I did not want seeing me standing there like a video geek in my Daffy Duck slippers.

Mrs. Tatum was leading me through the house to the white-tented backyard, right into the thick of the party. "How old are you, Karen?" Mrs. Tatum asked absently.

"Sixteen," I whispered, trying not to look at anybody. I could hear snickering, and I knew I wasn't being paranoid to assume it was at me.

"Oh. You're Nan's age. Do you two know each other?" I didn't get a chance to answer. "Nan, sugar, here's your friend Karen." Nan poked her head out from a cluster of fans, then disappeared again.

"I'm speaking with a few of my guests, Mother. Be there in a minute."

My mind clicked into overdrive. I could pretend I was sick, then wait for Mom in the car till my mortification blew over, which would be sometime around 2010. A voice from my dreams stopped me cold.

"Hey, Kari." Connor materialized in front of me. He cocked his head and took in my slippers. "I like your choice of footwear."

"I was sort of in a hurry," I babbled, pulling my camera in front of me like my old security blanket, Mr. Cuddles.

"What's with the camera? Wait, don't tell me. You're doing an exposé on teens forced to dress up for boring Friday night bashes."

Boring? It looked incredible to me.

"Actually, it's a new FOX show: *Sweet Sixteen 911.* I'm following the medics who are sedating anyone caught doing the chicken dance. It could get ugly." Okay, well, my mouth was still working, even if the rest of me was comatose with embarrassment.

Connor laughed, and a warm, syrupy feeling bubbled in my veins. "You're pretty funny. You'll make a great director someday."

How was it that he could make me feel good even when I was so clearly in the wrong place at the wrong time? Why was he even talking to me?

"Anyway, I'm glad you're here."

Stop the presses. Connor was glad to see me? Had they run out of people to mock? I was making myself a little dizzy. "You are?" I murmured.

Connor looked around, leaned in, and lowered his voice. "Yeah. I mean, this party is in danger of flat lining. All these Sweet Sixteens are the same. The girls

play princess. There's a spastic DJ with a wedding playlist. The food gets catered by Levenger's or The Manor. Big cake-cutting ceremony. Lots of Polaroid shots. And then parting gifts. So . . . unoriginal."

"Right," I said, not because I knew any better, but because I wanted him to keep leaning over me.

Jen Appleton was getting an eyeful of Connor and me from the dining room. A minute later Nan stood beside her, giving me that small, pained look girls get when they can't decide how to wring your neck without coming off as too mean. When I looked back again, Nan was nowhere to be seen and Jen was right beside me. The old send-in-the-second-in-command trick. Jen would cut me down while Nan stayed safely, sweetly in the background. True to form, Jen barreled right in between Connor and me.

"Connor. Nan wanted me to tell you that she's gonna cut the cake now."

Connor flashed me a knowing look. "What did I tell you?"

"Excuse me?" Jen snapped.

"I'll be there in a minute," Connor said, arms crossed.

"Connor," Jen whined. "You have to be there when she cuts the cake. It's a moment. And you're her boyfriend . . . of the moment," she added, like a threat.

"You can cut it out, Jen. I'll go when I'm ready."

Sigh. Connor had traveled beyond babedom. He was approaching godlike status.

Jen changed tack and turned to me. "So. What are you two talking about? It's Crystal, right?"

"Kari."

"Right. Did you find your invitation after all?"

A girl in a black, velvet Jessica McClintock dress spoke up. "Isn't your mom the fortune-teller?"

Oh, God. There it was. The weirdo connection again. I didn't get a chance to answer. Jen had taken the stick and was running with it faster than Fric and Frac on a good day.

"That's your mom? The lady who was putting party food in her purse?"

My usual smart-aleck defenses were down. I opened my mouth, but nothing came out. Instead Connor did the talking.

"Hey, Jen. Isn't that your broomstick double-parked outside? Maybe you should move it."

Jen didn't even register the dis. "I mean, does your mom really believe all the hoodoo guru stuff, or is it all an act?"

There was no way to answer that. I was starting to deflate.

"She seems nice," the black-velvet girl said, shrugging.

"Oh, I'm sure she's really, really *nice,*" Jen said with emphasis. Sometimes there's no greater insult in the world than *nice*. "But anyway, is that why you're here? To turn the cards for her? Or are you, like, getting some home movies?"

I don't know what came over me. There's just so much humiliation a girl can take before she snaps. I was tired of being thought of as an Odd Dobbins. I was sick of being treated like a joke. The time had come for action, even not-so-well-thought-out action.

"I'm making a documentary!" I blurted out, wondering where the words had come from even as I said them.

Jen looked clueless over the five-syllable word usage.

"A movie. I'm making a movie about Sweet Sixteen parties for my application to film school." I was? I mean, I was! I didn't know where the idea came from, but the longer my words floated in the air, the more I liked them.

Maybe it was my imagination, but the place seemed to get quieter. People were listening to me like I actually had something to say. So I just kept saying it. My mouth had a will of its own. "I've got some footage from a few parties in Charleston and one in Atlanta. From all over, really. People just keep inviting me. I've got some really interesting stuff."

Connor gave me that killer smile. "Well, check you out!"

The student body president, a guy named Ted Hodges, spoke up. "What a cool project. You thought that up yourself?"

Yeah, right this minute, in fact.

I nodded. "I haven't decided yet whether I'm going to NYU, USC, or UCLA. I guess it depends on how this turns out. I've been talking to them, and they're really into it." It was such a bogus thing to say, I couldn't believe it leaped out of my mouth.

"It's cool the way you just go after what you want, Kari," Connor said appreciatively, as if fifteen other people weren't suddenly listening in on the conversation. "Can I get you a Coke or something?"

"Sure," I managed. The happiness was so huge and sudden, I wasn't sure what to do with it.

Velvet Girl pulled me aside. "Would you come to my party and do the document thing? It's next month."

A redhead from the basketball team yelled to me from across the patio. "Mine too. It's not till July, though. Is that too late?"

What had I gotten myself into? I wanted to salvage my pride, not start a revolution. But I have to admit, the attention wasn't exactly unpleasant.

One of the cheerleaders tapped me on the shoulder. "I'd love for you to come to my party. It's in May. Maybe

we could hang out at school this week and talk about it."

Jen was still eyeing me like chicken gone bad. "So who's starring in your movie?"

"Well, um, actually," I began, "there is no star in a documentary. It's supposed to be a real slice of life about farmers in Idaho or blues musicians or, you know, Sweet Sixteen parties."

A guilty feeling was spreading through my gut. I'd crossed over the line from creative butt saving into full-fledged lying. Before I could feel totally icky, though, an idea buzzed in my brain.

Why couldn't I do a documentary of a Sweet Sixteen party? More important, why couldn't I do a documentary of my own Sweet Sixteen party? A film about a Sweet Sixteen would be a great way to make myself stand out on my college applications. And if it was a documentary, I wouldn't have to worry about scripts or rehearsals or any of that stuff. I'd even have a chance to show Connor that not all Sweet Sixteen parties were boring and unoriginal. I was going to throw a cool party. No cheesy Polaroid shots. No lame DJ. All it would take was careful planning. And that was my specialty.

"Well," Jen said, crossing her arms. "If you're so into this Sweet Sixteen documentary thing, how come you didn't have one yourself?"

It was the perfect lead-in. "Actually, it's in the works," I heard myself saying. "I've been, uh, getting the details together." I was buying time now. I needed to get home and make a list, to plan my attack. For the first time that evening I was feeling really, genuinely hopeful. I couldn't help adding, "That's where I'll be interviewing people about, like, who they are, what they want to be, what it's like being sixteen. That kind of stuff."

Velvet Girl was beside herself. "You *have* to invite me!"

"That does sound really cool," said a girl in an elegant green shift.

"Hey, don't forget about us," a varsity baseball guy yelled from his cluster of buddies.

Even Jen was getting in on the act now that half her peer group was psyched. She tucked her hair behind her ear and spoke in a low, sugary voice. "Listen, don't tell Nan, but I really wanted her to invite you tonight. I mean, if it had been up to me, I definitely would have. Keep me posted about the movie, 'kay?"

Connor sneaked up on me in that ultrasmooth way of his and handed me my soda. "I hope I make the list," he said, and gave me those puppy dog green-grays. My heart screamed, *You* are *the list.*

"Guess we'll see," I said, raising my glass of Coke in a toast and taking a sip. I missed, and Coke dribbled

down my chin. I wiped it really quickly and hoped he hadn't noticed. I put down my glass and hoisted my camera onto my shoulder like I'd done a million times before. Only this time it felt different, like I was somebody else. "I'm just gonna get a few shots of my mom," I said sheepishly.

"That's cool. You'll get to have your own mom in your film. Nice."

Okay, now I felt a little smarmy about the whole I'm-making-a-documentary thing. Maybe I wasn't a good enough person to go out with Connor. "Yeah, it is," I said, hoping my skin wasn't getting all hot and blotchy. "Well, gotta get to work."

I tossed back my hair and tried to act like I really knew what I was doing. Kari Dobbins. Together filmmaker. Cool chick. Nonfreak.

It wasn't so impossible. With some planning I could put together a Sweet Sixteen party that was so amazing, people would have to reevaluate the Dobbins family. I'd make my dad proud.

Salvation was only one party away. I just had to convince my mom to let me have it.

Mom was laying the wu-wu on pretty thick with one of the chaperons, a middle-aged lady in a sequined

dress that practically screamed "former prom queen." In contrast, my mom had on what I called her gypsy moth outfit: layers of colorful, wrinkled skirts and tunics, beads and bangles, and a hot pink Indian print T-shirt wrapped around her head like the top of an ear swab. Mom leaned forward and took the sequined lady's hand in hers.

"Louisa. Do you have gallstones?"

Louisa seemed to think Mom was moving too far into the personal space for comfort. She put her hands on her lap. "Gallstones? I don't think so. Doesn't it say anything about what my husband is buying me for our anniversary?"

Nice to know the tarot was being consulted about such earth-shattering issues.

"The cards are telling me something, Louisa. Something important. Why don't you try shuffling them again so they can pick up more of your energy?"

Louisa did as she was told. Mom introduced me without losing her concentration. "This is my daughter. She's just getting this on tape for my out-of-town clients."

Whenever we get some, I thought.

Louisa smiled at me, then shuffled the cards with her eyes closed, transferring all her energy to them.

I crouched down in the grass and zoomed out a bit

to make my mom look a little larger than life and mysterious. Actually, she was pretty mysterious as it was. Mom's astrology/tarot/psychic reading business had been officially under way for six months and unofficially since forever. I think she kept getting bookings because she confused people so much, they had to ask her back for another chance to explain. It wasn't that she was bad or anything; she was just weird at it. She picked up on strange things. Like if you asked whether it would rain on your birthday, she'd tell you your dog needed to go to the vet.

I could tell she was working the old bizarre Dobbins' spell on Louisa, who finished the most thorough shuffling of a deck I'd ever seen. Mom held the cards for a second or two, then turned over the top one.

"Three of Cups. This is what crosses you—your obstacle. It's inverted, upside down." Peering through the lens, I could see the eagerness on Louisa's face. Cameras are cool that way. They pick up everything a person is feeling. "You want the wrong thing. You're asking him for the wrong thing, Louisa." Mom sat back with this look of triumphant calm on her face.

In the lens Louisa's twitching was getting worse. "I just want the tennis bracelet I saw at Jim Murray Jewelers. What's wrong with that?"

"The cards don't fool around. This card says that wanting things, being too ambitious, gets in your way. Ask your husband to bring you wildflowers instead. You might get more than you wanted that way."

Louisa was burning a hole in the cards, looking for an answer. "So . . . if I ask Jim for flowers, he'll bring that *and* the tennis bracelet? I don't understand."

I stopped filming. This reading was going nowhere fast. I wished my mom would just tell her what she wanted to hear so she'd leave feeling satisfied and gossip to her lunch friends about how legit Mom's talent was. Then maybe her business wouldn't seem so . . . out there.

"You will understand, Louisa. I'm sure of it." Mom started shuffling the cards into a big, messy pile. "Oh, and have Dr. Grissom look at those gallstones. Don't forget!" Louisa finally clued in that it was time to go. She dropped a ten-dollar bill into Mom's tip jar and headed out of the tent, looking a little dazed.

I plopped into her chair, trying not to let my nervous energy show.

"Hi, sweetie. How was everything at home?"

"The same," I said, shrugging. I needed to slip the party stuff in under the radar. If I got too keyed up about it, Mom would start second-guessing and want to do a big astrological/numerological chart to see if the

idea was "psychically sound." "I started filling out my college applications."

Mom grabbed her humongous purse and poked her face in. "That's nice, dear."

No bells had gone off. So far, so good. "Actually, it's really tough. Most kids have a ton of honors and awards to show off." I waited for the standard Mom response of, "You're special in my eyes, honey." It didn't come. I cleared my throat. "Can I tell you my idea?" Mom nodded and pulled a peanut butter and mayonnaise sandwich from her bottomless purse, stimulating my hurl reflex. I could see the carrot and celery sticks Jen had mentioned tucked in Mom's purse in a little plastic bag. I could imagine Mrs. Tatum telling Mom to take some food home to her family, and I felt ashamed.

I took a deep breath before I went on. "Well, I kind of need a project to submit to make me stand out from the crowd, you know? So I'm making a documentary about teen rituals, like dating and pep rallies and Sweet Sixteen parties. Isn't that a great idea?"

"Mmmhmmpf," she mumbled through a mouthful of sticky sandwich.

It was time to go in for the kill. I blew the next sentence out in one breath. "So you can see why it's essential that I have a Sweet Sixteen party, then, right?"

Mom didn't look up. "But you turned sixteen in March."

"Yeah, I know," I snarled. My birthday had included some decoupage wall hangings from Lila's boyfriend du jour and a meal that can only be described as "experimental" from Mom. No fanfare. No cute boys. No big deal.

Mom picked up on the sad-sack tone in my voice. She patted my hand and left a thin streak of mayo on my knuckles. Can I just say bleccchhhh? "Sounds great, honey. We'll get an ice-cream cake; you can invite Jared and Dee over. Very nice."

Strike one. "That's not really what I had in mind. I was thinking more along the lines of a . . ."—I almost said *normal party*—". . . of a big party. You know, with food platters and beverages and a new dress. Something to really stand out on film . . ."

"Oh. Oh, gosh, Kari, honey. I don't know. We're Lila's guests. . . ." Strike two: the old backpedaling routine. Then would come, "Let's see what the cards say." Then the idea would be lost forever. I was not going to let my chance disappear.

"Mom. She's your mother. My grandmother. And we're not guests. We've been living there for four years. Embrace it."

"But it's awfully expensive. We couldn't afford a party like this one."

"I could put together a whole plan for doing it on the cheap. You know I can. And I was thinking. . . . What if I made a nice video brochure for your business? I mean soup to nuts, put the whole thing together. Then you could use some of your new biz money to pay for the party. What do you think?"

Mom sneaked a card off the top of her tarot deck, peeked at it, then stuck it inside the deck somewhere. "I think it's a great idea. But sweetie, you have to try to be nice to Lila if you want to do this. Get her involved, and she'll be a real pussycat about it. I know her."

"Sure, no prob," I said. I had no intention of getting Lila or any of my family involved. This was my show, and I needed it to go off without a hitch.

When it was all over, I'd have a film in the can, a new reputation, and maybe even a chance at Connor.

"You're doing what?" Jared, apparently, wasn't totally behind the party idea.

I looked around the mall to make sure no one had heard us. "Do you mind not completely wrecking my Barbie Dream House just yet? Sheesh, I haven't even planned the thing."

chapter 4

We walked past the Greenway Mall's atrium. A rock garden waterfall trickled down over polished stones. A knockoff of a knockoff of a Beatles song wafted out of the mall's hidden speakers.

"I'm sorry," Jared said, straight-faced. "What I meant to say was, 'Wow. A Sweet Sixteen party. Can I invite Muffy and Biff, and then we'll all have a hayride!' "

I wanted to be mad at him, but true to form, he got me laughing instead.

"Uh-oh," he said, grabbing my arm. "Mall-hair alert at two o'clock. I'm frightened, Auntie Em, I'm frightened!" He gave me his best Dorothy voice. Jared was a big *Wizard of Oz* fan. The winged monkeys were what made him want to draw in the first place. The sight of all those flying monkeys had scared the pee out of him as a kid. Drawing was his way of making the bad things disappear. "Let's grab a 'dog. I'm starving."

We scanned the mall's notorious food court and decided on maximum damage: giant corn dogs and frosty malts. Jared nabbed us a table by an overgrown fern. I rested my video cam on my lap.

"So," he said between bites. "Have you asked Lila the Horrible about your Sweet Sixteen plan of death?"

"My mom's handling it."

Jared feigned shock. "I'm sorry. While I was sleeping, did your mom grow a backbone?"

I punched Jared on the arm. Sometimes he could really cross the line with me. It was okay for me to talk about my family like that, but not him. "Cut it out. She's not that bad." Actually, my mom was every bit that bad. The last time she'd stood up to somebody was the eight-year-old paperboy who kept throwing our paper into the neighbor's yard.

"I think this whole Sweet Sixteen thing sounds like a recipe for disaster."

I leveled the video camera at him. "Why's that?"

Jared put his hand up like he was avoiding the paparazzi. Then he stuck his face right up in the lens.

"Hmmm, I don't know. Could it be because of your wacko family?"

I glared at him. It was a mean thought, but a thought I needed to consider. Could I really throw a well-controlled party amid the pure chaos that was my family? Could I really see introducing Isis, Theo, and Lila to Connor and half the sophomore class?

"You did think about that, didn't you?" Jared asked, polishing off his milk shake.

"Of course I did," I said, sounding totally defensive. I started thinking out loud. "I'll . . . just make sure they're not home when I have the party. You know, send them off to the movies or bowling or something."

"Bowling? What size shoes will George the iguana wear?" Jared snickered.

"Stop it," I snapped. I didn't mean to blow my cool, but I was starting to freak a little.

"You're cute when you're angry," Jared said.

"I'm not angry."

"No, you just bit my head off because you needed the protein. Speaking of, are you gonna finish that corn dog?"

I pushed my plate toward him.

"Actually, you can't get rid of Lila or your mom. At least one of them has to be there to chaperon."

He was right, of course. But I was starting to get

really annoyed with him. Who was he to criticize my family like that? Why did he have to be so negative all the time?

"What if they surprise you?" I asked.

"Nothing your family does could ever surprise me."

"What if they did? What if I gave them a makeover? Changed them into seminormal humanoids? Maybe they're not as hopeless as you think," I said stiffly. "It's just one night, after all."

Jared nearly choked on my corn dog. "Exactly!"

"Jared, *seriously*." No one believed I could do anything. I needed someone to believe in me. I needed to win. "Twenty bucks says I can pull it off—the party, the family, the film. . . ." *The Guy,* I added silently.

Jared leaned back in his chair and stared at me. "What?"

"What *what?*" I asked innocently.

The truth was, I had allowed myself a little daydream about inviting Connor Reese to my party. I guess I looked pretty moony.

"It's definitely something."

"It's nothing," I warbled unconvincingly.

I tried to change the subject. I wasn't ready to share my crush news with Jared. "We should go. The food court remains are ooging me out."

Jared anchored himself to his orange vinyl seat.

"What's with the mysterious? Come on, Kar. I told you about the time I sang a Whitney Houston tune at the church talent show, complete with an interpreter for the deaf. I think anything you could tell me is safe."

I don't know why I confessed. I guess I wanted somebody—a guy somebody—to tell me I was pretty and cool enough to merit the attention of a babe. Big mistake. "Well, you know Connor Reese?"

Jared looked thoughtful. "Tall. Doofy smile. Wears nice threads. That Connor Reese?"

"He does not have a doofy smile," I corrected. "And if you tell another living soul about this, I swear I will come film you in a drool state and post it on the Internet."

Jared made an *X* over his chest with his index finger. "Cross my heart."

"Well, I'm going to ask Connor to my party."

Jared shrugged and threw his empty cup at the trash can. It went in. "And . . . ?"

"I've sort of got this major crush on him. What do you think?"

Jared swallowed hard. "Doesn't he have an *über*witch girlfriend? Nan something or other?"

"I get the feeling they're sort of on the outs."

"People like that are always on the outs. Then they're

on the ins. No offense, Kar, but aren't you aiming a little out of your league?"

Ouch. I could practically feel my big nose and my sideshow family casting the world's largest shadow. A hard, tight ball squeezed against my throat. "What's that supposed to mean?"

"Look, I happen to like girls who are different looking."

Different looking? Thank you very much.

Mr. Sensitive kept right on. "But Connor. He strikes me as your basic Noxema Girl type. Nan Whatsername. Jen Appleton." He took a pause. "Dee." Double ouch. "That's not exactly you, Kar."

Jared had a way of getting under your skin with the truth. He saw everything you tried to hide. That's what made him such a good comic book artist. His heroes had flaws, and his villains had good traits. I just wished he could let me slide for once.

"Look, forget I said anything, okay? Are we getting your ear pierced today? Or did you bring me here solely to remind me that I'm a hopeless loser?"

"Let's motor." Jared did his version of speed walking toward the end of the mall.

I lagged behind by a few feet and willed my eyes not to produce tears. I had a strict rule about not crying in broad daylight in a place where people could buy anything they wanted.

A sign in front of the Merle Norman cosmetics store read Ears Pierced, 10–5.

"Can I he'p you, honey?" The woman behind the makeup counter was smiling at me. She was dressed in floral print from head to toe, giving her the unfortunate appearance of an overstuffed easy chair. "We've got some nice little pearl studs that'd be real pretty on you, sugar."

At least someone thought *pretty* and *me* belonged in the same sentence.

"I—ah—," I stammered.

"Actually, it's for me," Jared interrupted.

The chintz woman looked momentarily stunned. Boys wanting earrings probably wasn't covered in the Merle Norman customer service manual.

"Well. All right, then. You are over eighteen, aren't you?"

"Of course," Jared lied.

The woman, whose name tag read Betty Sue, pulled a needle gun out of a glass cabinet and wiped it down with alcohol. Then she grabbed a pen and cocked Jared's head to one side. "I'm just marking your earlobe with a little dye. It'll wash off. I sure hope your parents know what you're doing."

"Oh yes. Indeedy . . . Betty Sue."

Betty Sue smiled like the Rose Queen and patted Jared's arm. Then she leaned in conspiratorially. "You aren't doing this to impress some girl, are you, honey?"

Jared's eyes glanced in my direction, then locked onto Betty Sue's face. "No. Definitely not an impress-the-girl thing. Unless you know someone?"

"Oh, you are funny!" Betty Sue got serious. "'Cause you do know this is permanent. I mean, the hole can close over someday, but you'll always have a mark there. I just think you should know that before I pierce you."

Jared snorted. "So it's okay to maim girls for life, but you want to make sure boys think about it first. Gotcha."

I knew he was making a joke, but to the un-Jared initiated, it sounded kind of mean.

Betty Sue pulled back her hand and picked up a tray of small silver and gold studs from the counter behind her. She put the tray down hard. "Girls need accessories," she said with a sniff. "Pick out your earring."

Jared scanned the black velvet tray, then pushed it toward her. "These leave me a little . . . cold. Is this your whole selection?"

Betty Sue was clearly tired of playing. She brought out a huge tray of earrings from the back. It was a cornucopia of tackiness. Mermaids dangled from golden filigree chains. Big, chunky cubic zirconia flowers glared at us. There were rainbows. Unicorns. Yin-yang signs. Even a pair of chubby, sad-eyed angels.

Jared gave me an appraising glance. "What do you think?"

My hand hovered for a minute, then hit pay dirt. "It's you," I said, handing him a small, leaping silver dolphin silhouette.

Jared smiled and gave me a fake hug. His arms were thicker than I remembered somehow. More muscular. "This speaks to my tribe, kemo sabe."

Betty Sue looked up from color coordinating the eye shadows. "Are you an Ind—Native American?"

Jared's eyes twinkled. "On my dad's side."

"I thought you looked like you might have some Indian blood in you. I saw *Dances with Wolves* five times. You got an Indian name like that?"

"Yes. Plays with Matches."

"Isn't that something? What tribe?"

"Winnebago," Jared said with a straight face. "We're a nomadic race. Listen, I'd love to talk tomahawk with you, but my lovely wife and I are late to a powwow. The piercing marks my transition from a boy to a man, and we can't wait to celebrate. Here you go . . . one dolphin."

Betty Sue adjusted her floral shift for the big moment, and I felt a little sorry for her. Jared was always making up weird stories to make his family seem more interesting. I was always trying to bury my weird family stories in search of the boring and normal.

Betty Sue fixed Jared with her piercing gun. "This will just sting a bit. . . ." There was a staple sound, and when she pulled back, Jared's ear was flushed red with a small silver outline at the tip.

It looked good, like it had been there forever and I'd only just noticed. After promising to send Betty Sue a postcard from a tribal dance festival in Wyoming, Jared and I pushed out into the throngs of shoppers. I swerved toward Radio Shack.

"Come on. I need to buy some videotape," I said, pulling Jared into the brightly lit store. He twirled and broke my grip. "It'll only take a sec, okay? In and out."

Radio Shack was hopping. A sale on cellular phones had brought in every weekend warrior in town. I grabbed a two-pack of high-grade tape and headed for the counter.

A hand clapped down on my shoulder. "I saw you take that. Better put it back, or I'll have to run you in, young lady." I turned and faced the hulking ex-marine behind me.

"Hi, Mr. Jameson. How are you?"

He laughed, and his flinty eyes crinkled. "Fine. You teaching my son some manners today?" He looked over at Jared. He was smiling, but his jaw was set. "You got your work cut out for you. Hello, Jared. Hey, I'm talking to you, son."

"Yes, sir," Jared said, taking a sudden interest in a sale bin of telephone cords.

Mr. Jameson put his arm around my shoulders and hugged me. "I keep telling Jared he needs to invite you over. If I had a girlfriend as pretty as you, I'd take her everywhere and show her off. Of course, if Jared would help me out at the store here some nights 'stead of sitting in his room drawing comic books, he might have enough greenbacks to take you out on a proper date." He laughed the way people do when they're sharing a joke that's anchored in meanness deep down.

Jared looked thoroughly miserable.

I was digesting what Mr. Jameson had just announced. He'd said *girlfriend*. As in friend who is a girl. As in . . . really? Was that why Jared had been so schizoid around me? Were we making that awkward hormonal jump from punching each other on the arm to long, meaningful stares and hurt, reproachful silences? My mind started scripting the movie without the rest of me totally participating: Best buds fall passionately in love after he finally confesses his love for her.

I looked at Jared, but before I could agonize over the

topic, Jared put the kibosh on the whole me-him idea.

"Dad, Kari is not my girlfriend, okay? I mean, Kari and me? Please." Okay, he didn't have to be quite so final about it. I didn't want to go out with Jared any more than he wanted me, apparently. But did he have to dismiss me so quickly? My ego couldn't take much more squashing.

Mr. Jameson took my videotapes and scanned them. "Whatever you say, son. That's three eighty-three. Family discount." He winked.

I paid, and Jared grabbed the bag. "Let's go, Kari. We gotta run, Dad." Jared turned to the left, and Mr. Jameson's smile hardened into a grimace.

"What the . . . ?" He marched over to Jared and whirled him around. The dolphin earring caught the light, then dove into darkness again. Jared's dad brought his voice down to a harsh whisper. "I oughta whup you right here. Would serve you right."

"Dad . . ."

"You look like a sissy. Take it out right now." Mr. Jameson held his sizable paw out for the earring. Jared clenched and unclenched my bag of videotapes in his hand. Mr. Jameson grabbed a fistful of Jared's Silver Surfer T-shirt. Jared brought his arm up reflexively, trying to unhook himself, but his dad had him snared.

I knew I should say something, yell "fire" or make a

lousy joke or jump on Mr. Jameson's broad back, kicking and screaming, but I couldn't seem to move. Emotion has a way of immobilizing me. Fortunately a man in a polo shirt cleared his throat.

"Excuse me . . . Can I get some help over here?"

Mr. Jameson snapped to attention. "Be right with you, sir." He pointed a threatening finger at Jared as he walked away. Words weren't needed. Jared walked out of Radio Shack without saying anything. I ran after him.

"Jared!" I half yelled. He stopped, and I caught up with him. "He's a jerk, okay?"

"Ah, but he's my jerk. Isn't that what I'm supposed to say with love in my voice?"

I didn't know what to tell him. My dad was the best, but he existed only in memories. Jared's dad was alive and a terrible pain. Please see listing under life is unfair.

"Hey, Jared. I thought that was you." A skinny guy with glasses walked up to us. I'd seen him around. He was a senior whose folks owned a print shop. He looked down at the see-through bag of videotapes Jared was still clutching tightly. "Planning to tape a year's worth of *Ally McBeal*?"

I broke in. "It's mine. I'm making a video documentary."

"Impressive. Hey, Jared, you never told me you were

friends with the future Tarantino." The skinny kid gave me a once-over.

Ick. Just my luck to have the president of Future Backgammon Players of America want me.

"Must've slipped my mind. We've really gotta run, Mark."

Obnoxious Boy wasn't budging. "I'm Mark, by the way. I'm a business associate of Jared's."

"Hi. I'm Kari," I said quickly.

Mark tilted back his head and looked at me strangely. "So you're Kari . . . of Kari and Dee fame."

Dee. Wow. So Jared had been talking about Dee. Dee, Dee, Dee . . . Dee? Oh. My. God. That must be it—Jared had the hots for Dee. Suddenly I couldn't bring myself to look at my best buddy. This was turning into a whole new dimension of awkward.

Apparently Jared felt it, too. "I'll meet you at the car. Aisle B-22," he said, and took off at a race-walk clip for the exit.

"Nice to meet you," I mumbled. Mark was still looking at me strangely. *I'm entering a convent for big-nosed loser girls, so go away,* I wanted to shout after him.

Jared and I pushed through the exit doors into the afternoon sun, letting it thaw our goose-pimply skin.

Jared and Dee. I had to admit that it was hard to

think of my two favorite people becoming an item. But when I saw how tense Jared looked, I had an idea that suddenly filled me with optimism.

Just because I was the dateless wonder didn't mean other people couldn't be happy. Dee was . . . perfect for Jared. Really. She was sweet and loving and romantic. She would gaze at him in a way that would nauseate entire cafeteria tables full of budding Romeos. She would feel about him the way I felt about Connor.

What this lovesick movie needed was a director. Enter me. Hey, if I could get those two together, it might give me the kick I needed to put together a romance of my own. I would call the beauteous Miss Deirdre the minute I got home and concoct some reason she had to hang with me. The romance of Jared Jameson and Deirdre "Dee" Malloy would be my greatest triumph, next to enchanting Connor Reese, getting a full scholarship to NYU, and turning my family into a Sears portrait of normalcy. Things were looking up.

Jared was yelling to me from the car. "Are you coming in this century?" The sun was low and runny in the sky. I gazed out and saw my best friend's black-clad form bathed in an orangy glow, like a Bedouin warrior.

"Yeah," I said, running toward him. "Hold your horses, Plays with Matches."

chapter 5

Dee and I had been friends since the time in sixth grade when we'd been forced to do a rap version of Betsy Ross making the flag. That kind of total humiliation tends either to bond people for life or force them into early therapy. Friendship is cheaper.

On the surface Dee and I were a combo like peanut butter and goat cheese. But somehow it worked. Dee needed a little direction. I needed a little mellowing at times.

I wish I could say I was having no trouble with Dee's recent metamorphosis from gawky to gaga. As a freshman, Dee was as geeky as Jared and I, trying out for a majorette position with her glitter baton. Glasses. Braces. Then over Christmas break came "the body." I swear, she developed faster than one-hour film. She followed that up with contacts and a new smile, and suddenly Dee was a swan. But Dee being Dee, she was a swan with a band geek heart.

"Here we go," Dee trilled as we neared town in the Jesus mobile. It was just dusk when Dee and I hit

Greenway's infamous "strip," a one-mile stretch of road flanked on either side by every fast-food restaurant and covert teen meeting spot in town. Ordinarily I didn't go for this kind of mindless release of pent-up teenage lust. I'd rather watch James Dean act out for me in *Rebel Without a Cause*. But I was on a mission. I had coaxed Dee into driving the Jesus mobile while I filmed a Saturday night on the strip as part of my documentary. At least, that's the story I gave her.

"I'm so psyched I get to be in your movie!" Dee squealed. She's a big squealer. I try to overlook it. "Does my hair look okay?"

What hair I could see under a rain forest of meticulously placed butterfly clips looked big and bouncy and shampoo-commercial perfect.

"You look great," I said. "Go slow so I can get a good shot of all the cars."

A Ford pickup with mag wheels slowed down even with us. A beefy guy leaned out the truck's window. He had a mouthful of chewing tobacco. "Hey. How you ladies doin' tonight?"

"He's kinda cute." Dee giggled. Did I mention Dee is also a giggler? She took a quick look in the side mirror to fix her hair.

Chaw Boy spoke again. "I'm Terry. This here's Jay.

What do you say we meet at Hunter's Point?" Hunter's Point is the local makeout spot. Or so I'd heard.

"I don't think . . . ," I started, but Dee shouted over me.

"Only if you can catch us!" The light turned green, and she gunned the motor, giving Jesus and his disciples a taste of a V-6 engine. To my amazement, the Jesus mobile actually responded without stalling. We went sailing into the night, leaving Terry and Jay in our wake. "Hold on," Dee yelled, making a sudden left turn across oncoming traffic and into the safety of the Sonic drive-in. She pulled up to an order box and cut the engine.

"Did you get that on tape?"

"Uh, I can't remember much after the whiplash set in," I said.

The order box squawked into action. "Two cherry limeades," Dee answered. "Whew. All that James Bond stuff makes a girl thirsty."

A limeade lackey brought us our drinks. Outside, a parade of cars passed behind us, looking for relief from Saturday night boredom. I took a deep breath. "So, Dee, I was just wondering. . . . What do you think of Jared?"

"Jared? Why?" Her eyebrows snapped together. "What have you heard?"

"Nothing! Paranoid much? I was just thinking that y'all might make a cute couple, that's all." I tried to sound very casual, like the idea had formed in my head while I was brushing my teeth.

Dee leaned forward and grabbed my arm. "Oh my God. You will not believe this, but I have this major, major crush on him, okay? Isn't that so Roswell?"

Roswell was Dee's term for anything she considered out of the ordinary, from having your math book disappear from your locker to two people discovering they shared the same dermatologist.

"Totally," I said. There was no need to mention the practice signature of Mrs. Jared Jameson I'd seen all over her Piggly Wiggly book cover in history. Of course, the signature was mixed in with Mrs. Just About Every Guy in the Tenth Grade, so who knew for sure? Still, there had been a big heart around it. "It's fate, then. I was at the mall today with Jared . . . and I'm pretty sure he wants to go out with you."

"Oh my God!" Dee's voice floated up to a frequency only dogs can hear. "This is so monumentally amazing. So why doesn't he ask me out?"

I thought about Connor. If only it were so easy. "Well, here's the thing: He wants to; he's just shy. You know how Jared is. He's usually holed up in his room with art supplies and a year's worth of comic books. He's not so good at the talking-relating thing."

"Should I call him? Ask him out?"

"No!" I answered, a little too forcefully. Then Jared would know I'd put her up to it. "I mean, we've got to plan it carefully. . . ."

A slightly familiar laugh drifted over the parking lot. Through the windshield I saw Nan Tatum's silver-blue convertible BMW, top down, in the parking spot catty-corner to the Jesus mobile. She was perched on the hood with her arms around Connor, who was wearing that superstylin' fedora of his. A tingle crept up my spine and electrified my whole rib cage. He bent in to kiss her forehead, and I swear I felt his breath on my face, warm and moist. I was torn between the desire to gawk at them and the impulse to look away. It was like a highway accident.

I brought up the camera and centered them in the zoom lens. They came into perfect focus, and I felt a chilling numbness. I was fooling myself to think that Connor would ever be interested in an outsider like me.

"What are you looking at?" Dee asked.

"Nothing. Just practicing," I replied, not taking my eyes off the scene. I needed to torture myself, to sear the truth into my brain.

Nan's friends were sitting in the backseat. Jen Appleton flopped into the front seat and half climbed over the windshield. She put her cigarette in Nan's mouth, and Nan took a drag, exhaling a wispy puff of smoke.

Connor looked angry. He said something and stepped back from Nan, who had a hold on his turquoise 1950s bowling shirt. I realized he wasn't happy about the icky nicotine puff. I zoomed in as far as I could go to see if I could read his lips. A waving hand came across my lens. I looked up and saw a girl in a tank top.

"Excuse me. Do you know where the party is tonight?"

"Sorry," I said. Great. Another party. Whoo-hoo.

The sound of a tray being slammed against a car door interrupted our conversation. When I looked back at the scene in parking spot number eleven, Nan was pushing Jen Appleton over and starting up the car.

"Fine! Forget you, then!" Nan screamed, backing out her Beamer and nearly crashing into a gray Camry. Connor had both hands on the front hood, trying to stop her.

I wondered what it would be like to have Connor Reese try to stop you from getting away from him. And I wondered what kind of fool would even try.

Nan's car lurched forward, and my heart stopped for a full three seconds. Connor jumped out of the way before he could become the world's sexiest hood ornament.

"Could I at least have my jacket?" he yelled.

A brown blur came flying over the back of the car

and hit the pavement, where the Camry ran over it. Nan tore out of the Sonic parking lot and into the now inky Greenway night.

I couldn't help feeling a little thrill when she left. It was like being in a hot room and having someone open the window a crack.

Connor put his hands on his hips and shook his head in that stoic Gary Cooper way of his. It reminded me of my dad—so quiet, calm, dignified. So . . . *there*. The sight of him bending down to pick up his filthy, ruined jacket made me want to run over and help him dust it off. At the same time I didn't really want him to see me like this, dateless on a prime weekend night, videotaping life from the safety of the Jesus mobile.

"Let's go," I said to Dee, shutting off the camera.

"Can you believe her? How rude can you be?"

"Yeah, it's tragic. I should get home."

"Kari, don't look now, but guess who's coming over?"

Common sense told me to keep my head down, but common sense wasn't exactly my strong suit. I raised my eyes and found Connor coming over to my window, wearing a sheepish grin. It looked good on him.

"Hi," he said, crouching down even with my face.

"Hi back," I said, turning my face three-quarters to minimize the nose that roared.

"Seen any good foreign dwarf movies lately?"

"Nothing but cheap Hollywood dwarf movies," I managed. His face was inches from mine. One wrong move and we would be touching. Or was that one right move?

"Hi, I'm Dee!" Dee stuck her hand past my face and out the window. Connor shook it graciously.

"Nice to meet you, Dee. I think we had chem together last quarter. Deacon's class?"

"Really? You remember me?"

"Yeah. Well, when your aspirin experiment went wrong and you made a small explosive, it was hard not to notice you."

"Oh, right," Dee said. Suddenly I wished Dee and her great body and butterfly hair clips were somewhere else. This was supposed to be my moment. Fireworks and "fancy meeting you here" and all that stuff.

"So . . . what are you up to?" What are you up to? Had I actually said that?

Connor gave me that cool half smirk of his. "Walking, apparently."

Should I acknowledge the fight I'd just witnessed? Pretend it didn't happen? I settled for the noncommittal. "Would you like a ride? We were just out getting some footage for my documentary." My documentary. I meant to toss it off with a hip oh-I-do-this-all-the-time

air. Instead I sounded like a seventh grader talking about her extra-credit project.

"That'd be great. Could you do me a favor?"

Anything. Everything. I'd walk over hot coals and change my name to Bambi with an *i*. "Sure," I said weakly.

"I was supposed to catch Robin's Hoods at Café Vortex tonight. Could you give me a ride over there?" Robin's Hoods was the hottest swing band in the South. They played the Vortex a lot. I could just imagine Connor jumping and jiving to a big band, sweat trickling down his sideburns, his well-loved wing tips flashing across the dance floor.

I made a mental note to buy every Robin's Hoods CD I could get my hands on. I'd also need to learn to dance. Well, developing any sense of rhythm would be a good idea. The last dancing I'd done was the hokey pokey at Jared's ninth birthday party.

"Robin's Hoods. I hear they're great," I said, like I knew what I was talking about.

"They smoke, man. Why don't you come with me and check 'em out?" Connor flashed that smile.

"You never told me you liked Robin's Hoods," Dee said to me. "I thought you said swing bands were too retro and derivative."

I laughed so loud, it came out my nose like a horse's

whinny. "Such a jokester, this one!" I leaned close to Dee and whispered through clenched teeth, "Don't you need to go home and help your mom with that big project?" I fixed her with a meaningful glance.

Dee returned the stare. It was like she was trying to read my mind through my skull. "What project? My mom's playing bridge with the Thomases. She always plays bridge on Saturdays."

I'd hate to be one of those lame-o girls who dumps her friend the minute a cute guy happens on the scene, but I was mighty tempted. This wasn't just any guy. It was Connor Reese, and he was sort of asking me out. Okay, so without me he'd be spending his Saturday night scarfing leftover Tater Tots while digging up cab fare, but why overanalyze?

"Hop in," I said. "Door's open."

Connor stepped back and appraised the car for the first time. A fresh wave of humiliation washed over me. "Wow. This is some car. Are your parents really religious?"

"They have unusual taste in cars." And houses. And clothes. And lives.

"Well, it's different," he said cheerfully, leaning forward so I could get a whiff of that clean smell. "Let's see what this puppy can do."

"Right," said Dee. She peeled out into the warm

spring night with Connor's "whoo-hoo!" sailing on the air. Car lights blinked all around us like Christmas Eve, and even though it was only April, it felt every bit like my favorite holiday had come early.

Café Vortex was definitely jumping by the time we got there. At first the manager didn't want to let me in. Something about the camera and thinking I worked for some ambush news show.

"Don't you know who this is?" Connor asked. Manager Man crossed his arms and didn't budge. "This is Kari Dobbins. She's gonna be going to the NYU film school, man. She's, like, a camera genius, and she wants to get a few shots of your club."

The boy was smooth. Manager Man gave me a critical once-over. "Dobbins. Hey, you're not related to that kid Theo who keeps bugging me to book his sorry band, are you?"

My stomach clenched. Every time I thought I'd run ahead of my family's rep, it was waiting around a corner to sack me.

Connor came to my rescue, slipping the guy a five-dollar bill. "Dude, don't you want the Vortex to be famous? Come on, man. Let her in."

The manager pocketed the five and opened the red velvet ropes for us. I loved the way Connor could make

things happen. He squeezed my arm on the way in. "Okay. Make me proud, Dobbins. I'm out a fiver."

A crush of dancers was tearing up the floor in front of the stage, and Robin's Hoods hadn't even started yet. There were a lot of out of towners, fans following the band from gig to gig. The guys were decked out in zoot suits. The girls wore 1940s dresses complete with heels and little white anklet socks. It was like a scene out of a movie. Inside the club's dark cave, I moved over by a big column and pointed my lens toward the dancers. Flying legs and arms darted in and out of focus—great practice for my Sweet Sixteen's action sequences. Hot swing pounded from the club's speakers. Connor handed me a banana-strawberry smoothie and pointed to a table in the back where we wouldn't have to shout over the music to be heard.

"So Kari," Connor said, pulling out a chair for me and then Dee. "Have you always wanted to make movies?"

"Ever since I can remember," I replied, trying to sound grown-up and sure of myself.

"Well," Dee added. "Except for that period in sixth grade when you said you were going to be a ballerina." I tried to kick Dee under the table but couldn't quite reach her.

"I think that is so cool," Connor said, sending my heart into orbit. "So what all have you done?"

Gulp. Right back to the NYU application. I didn't

want Connor to think I was a total poser. "W-W-Well." I was stuttering. Not good. Control, Kari. Stay in control. "Nothing that rocks my world yet. Practice stuff. You know, some mood pieces. A little bit of super eight."

"When did you do that?" Dee wanted to know. "I thought you said you'd only shot on video."

Dee was becoming a major cramp in my new style. To tell the truth, I had only worked on video. But I was planning to branch out very soon. Besides, eight millimeter had such a guerrilla sound to it. I fixed Dee with a don't-go-there look. "I don't tell you everything, you know. Mrs. Jameson."

Dee's eyes went huge, and she clammed up.

The lights dimmed a bit, and the crowd broke into spontaneous clapping and whooping. Connor stood up and craned his neck to see the stage. "Looks like the band's coming on."

The sound guy's voice came through the speakers. "Ladies and gentlemen, put your hands together for Robin's Hoods!" Eight guys in big suits and wing tips like Connor's bounded onstage. The lead singer counted one, two, three, and they launched into a high-energy song that had the dance floor mobbed. These guys really rocked. I could see why Connor and everybody else was so wild about them.

"Come on," Connor said, grabbing my hand. "Let's cut a rug."

I held back. "I don't know how to dance like that. You go ahead."

Connor gave me his hat. "Watch that for me?"

Watch it? I wanted to hug it. I even went so far as to give it a quick sniff. It had a warm, guy smell, like he'd been wearing it to rake leaves or start a campfire. I was falling in love with a scent.

Connor had found a partner and was twisting and twirling all over the floor. The boy could really move, which wasn't helping my crush. This was just the sort of teens-of-today footage that was going to make my film project jump up and say "pick me" at NYU.

Putting Connor's hat on my head for safekeeping, I fired up the video cam and got an eyeful of Connor Reese jitterbugging his way into my heart. I could have sat there watching him safely from behind my camera for hours. Honestly. But after three songs the band down-shifted into a mellow mood. The singer's ultrasmooth voice was laying it down about love being a funny thing.

"That hat looks good on you," Connor said, wiping a little sweat off his forehead.

I'd forgotten I was wearing it. "Oh. Sorry," I said, handing it over.

Connor put it back on my head. "No. Keep it on. It's you." I was glad it was dark because I could feel a cheesy, teenybopper grin stretching across my face. "How about a slow dance? No major moves required." He held out his hand, and I took it.

We made our way onto the packed dance floor and shifted from foot to foot mostly. I didn't care. Being this close to Connor made huge goose bumps pop up along my arms. I wanted to pay the band to keep playing that song all night.

A few minutes later the band launched into a fast one, and Connor led the way back to our table. We squeezed through the crowd and bumped right into Jen Appleton. Nan was nowhere to be found.

"Hi, Connor," Jen said, looking over his shoulder at me. "Have you seen Nan?"

"Not since she ran over my jacket about an hour ago. 'Scuse us." Connor pushed on through, but Jen blocked my path.

"How's the movie going?"

"Fine," I said, keeping an eye on Connor's head as it moved away.

"A couple of people at the party last night said this whole movie thing is bogus. That it's, like, an excuse to hang with us. Is it for real?"

I stopped. "Yeah, it's for real."

Jen smirked. I'd let her get under my skin, and she knew it.

I touched the brim of Connor's hat. "I'm probably going to enter it in some film festivals and stuff. You know, a lot of people have been discovered that way. Not just directors, but, like, actors and models and all." So outrageous, I should have been struck by lightning. Since I wasn't, I went for the kill. "But hey, if y'all don't want to be in it, that's cool."

Jen's eyes got big. She caught herself and sneered. "Discovered? Please."

I was starting to get a little desperate and ticked off. "Actually, a friend of my grandmother's might be coming to check things out. He's a casting director." It was such a stupid thing to say. I instantly wished I could take it back. Bingo. That was all Jen needed to hear.

"A casting director? For which network?"

My face went limp, like a tanking fish. My voice came out small and far away. "Network? Uh, I really shouldn't say, really." Really. Really shouldn't say.

Jen was off and running. "Ohmigod. Not the WB, is it? That's, like, my favorite channel in the whole universe. I can't believe you're so connected."

I was a bad person. I couldn't believe the stuff I'd said. But I mean, I hadn't really committed to anything, right?

"Listen, don't worry. I'll spread the word that you rate, okay?" Jen flounced off to a table in the corner.

I could practically feel the rumor mill turning as I walked back to our table, promising myself that I'd fix it all later.

"So, where do you live?" I asked, trying to sound casual as the Jesus mobile idled at a red light. We'd just dropped Dee off at her house and were finally alone.

"Foxcroft," Connor answered. "It's out Tanglew—"

"I know where it is," I said softly. It was deep in my neighborhood. The fashionable part.

"Great. Where's your house?"

"Skylark," I practically whispered.

"Wow," he said. "I can't believe we live in the same neighborhood."

Ordinarily that would have been cause for great celebration. But I didn't want Connor to make the association between me and the Freak Castle. Not till I'd had a chance to make it over.

"Listen, you don't have to drop me off. I can just walk from your house," Connor offered.

"Oh no," I said, too quickly. "No. I'll drive you home. It's no trouble."

"It's late. I can't let you drive home alone at night.

I'll walk. Besides, I want to see the house of the famous film director."

A thin layer of sweat was breaking out on my upper lip. We were approaching the turnoff for my—our—neighborhood. Maybe we'd have an accident. Nothing life threatening. Just something to delay the house tour thing.

"Oh, you know what? I should pick up milk for my mom. We're out. So I'll drop you and then go get it."

"Just pull into the Quickie Mart on the corner."

"I don't think they have milk." Beyond retarded. If there's life on Mars, you can be sure their Quickie Marts have milk.

Connor wasn't having it, either. "Call me wacky, but I think the mart is pretty well stocked with your average moo juice."

Busted. I pulled into the small parking lot and emerged from the Quickie Mart five minutes later with a gallon of milk we didn't need. I was out of excuses. I let the Jesus mobile lead me toward the moment of embarrassment. It had been a nice evening. Too bad.

As we inched slowly up the hill toward our house, I secretly hoped a streetlight had gone out and left it hidden by shadows. No such luck. It blossomed out of the street like a toadstool. I pulled into our driveway but left the engine running.

"You live here?" Connor asked incredulously. Lila's primitive yard gnomes stood like guards on either side of our weed-infested walkway. "It's very unique."

That was a nice way of putting it. I couldn't let him think we lived this way. "Oh, the wooden scary guys and the whole Elvis-meets-Frankenstein decor? That's left over from a piece I was shooting for my sister. She needed something fun for a Halloween party she was going to."

"Halloween was six months ago already."

"I know," I said, digging myself in deeper. "Mom keeps telling her to take it all down, but you know how little kids are. . . ." Isis would have pulled out all my teeth with pliers if she heard me call her a little kid. "Once they get attached to something, well, what can you do?"

"That's great that your mom still lets her play with it. My mom would have a style cow. She goes a little mental if you squeeze the toothpaste from the middle or mess up the pillows on the couch."

I drifted off, imagining such a normal, well-ordered household. "Sounds great . . . ," I said.

"It does?" Connor turned and looked at me, and I realized I'd forgotten to put that filter between my brain and mouth back in place again.

"I mean, sounds like a great place. You live on

Foxcroft, right?" I was making such an idiot of myself.

Connor gave me a hello-are-you-still-on-this-planet? look and said simply, "Right."

Foxcroft. I knew the street. It was five blocks over in the nicer part of our neighborhood, where people were renovating their old-fashioned bungalows like crazy. Connor's place was probably something out of *Better Homes & Gardens*. The kind of house I dreamed about.

Pathetic as it was, when I couldn't fall asleep at night, I'd lie in bed and overhaul our house from top to bottom. In my mind I'd throw out stacks and stacks of *Reptile World* magazines. I'd replace Isis's corkboard with a framed print and place a little table under it where a phone and answering machine would live permanently. I'd eighty-six the grody green-and-brown sofa, bring in the new cream slipcover. I'd say bye-bye to fuchsia bathroom walls and hello to tasteful wallpaper. I'd reorganize the kitchen, fix up the garden, donate the tiki torch and yard gods to a theme park. I'd plant impatiens on the front porch and chuck all those creepy snake cages.

Connor broke in on my Martha Stewart moment. "All that dancing made me thirsty. Would you mind if I came in and got a drink of water?"

Connor? Inside? "No!" I said, a little wildly. "I mean,

I'd invite you in, but my grandmother's already in bed. I don't want to wake her up."

"I wasn't planning on playing a drum solo. I just wanted a drink of water." He managed to make it sound sweet and flirty.

"It's not that. It's just . . ." What? What could I come up with that wouldn't sound like the biggest brush-off of all time? I didn't want Connor to think I was a water hoarder or that I didn't like him when I was absolutely, positively wacko for him. But if I let him into our house of horrors, I'd never live it down. He wouldn't see me, Kari Dobbins, together filmmaker. He'd see Kari the superfreak whose family belonged in a circus sideshow. "I have to study for my biology test."

Connor gave me a stunned face. "Biology test," he repeated. Even I couldn't believe I'd come up with such a ridiculous excuse.

"Right," I said. "So sorry. Look, I'll drive you home. It'll only take a nanosecond. Really." This was not going well.

"Kari, I know you're supersmart and all, but it's Saturday night. Can't you wait till tomorrow to study?"

"Uh . . ." I was sinking fast. "I have . . . something . . . to do tomorrow. I can't get out of it. So I have to study tonight."

There was a silence that followed my lame explanation. I can only describe it as painful.

"Sure, okay. Whatever," Connor said. He slumped down a little in his seat, and my hopes slumped with him. Cicadas sang outside in the grass, but no one was dancing. With a heavy heart, I backed out of my driveway. Connor started quietly humming a song to himself and looking out the window in that I-couldn't-care-less way that guys have a patent on. The three-minute drive to Connor's beautiful house seemed to take an hour. When he bounded out of the car with just a short "thanks," I wanted to crawl into a hole and never come out.

"Bye," I murmured, so softly even the car didn't hear me.

I was going home to my room to listen to Sarah McLachlan till my ears bled, till I was so far down in the dumps that even Hallmark couldn't make a card to reach me.

The headlights fell across my ramshackle yard. The snake cages. The bad paint job. The windows where Mom and Lila and Theo and Isis slept, unaware that I was plotting a future without them.

A twinge of guilt ignited, then quieted. I closed the car door and let myself into the darkened living room, knowing that tomorrow I would call and find a place to have my party. Somewhere far away from here.

chapter 6

The next morning dawned bright and clear to mock me. I thought about the sour end to my promising night with Connor and buried my head under the pillow. At ten o'clock Lila stood over my bed with her car keys in one hand and her pocketbook (she refused to call it a purse) in the other. "Rise and shine, Turpentine!"

"Am I dead?" I asked, peeling my pillow off my face. "Is this hell?"

"Don't be so dramatic, Kari Elizabeth." Lila had a thing for calling me by my full name. It was like I needed a middle name to become a serious person. Or maybe that was the only way she could remember who I was, like having to say your phone number really fast or you can't recite it.

"C'mon, get dressed. The day is burning. We're late."

I didn't remember having an appointment. "Late for what?"

"We have an appointment with destiny, also known as the caterer. For your party, darlin'. Now, let's go."

Caterer? Lila?

Lila went to fix her wig in my mirror. I swiped the to-do list I'd made the night before from my nightstand. *1. Tell Connor Theo had typhoid to explain behavior. Something. Anything. 2. Find normal place for party.*

I had been too depressed to finish the list. I hoped Lila hadn't seen item number two. A caterer, huh? It looked like Lila was coming through for me after all. I wanted to see the look on Jared's smug face when I told him.

I jumped out of bed, feeling forgiveness in my heart. Brushing my teeth and hair in a hurry, I let myself imagine a quaint, old-fashioned place that served up miniature quiches, petit fours, and a big, scene-stealing cake. Something elegant. Refined. Sophisticated. I sighed. It was like a dream come true.

Lila drove us to the end of the earth, about fifteen miles outside of town to a place called Tokyo Joe's BBQ. It's that combination sushi-barbecue joint the world has been clamoring for. Lila had radar for this kind of thing.

My mood was heading a little south. So much for refined. I tried not to get bent out of shape. There was always the chance that the food was incredible. Or that they were some exclusive outfit based in New York or something. It could happen.

Tokyo Joe himself met us at the door. "Howdy, pardner," he said, ushering us inside. "Have a seat."

Lila dropped into a big chair with cow cushions and a back painted like a cactus. I took a look around. It was Lila decor, for sure. Every wall had miles of Hollywood studio stills featuring Western stars. John Wayne. Gene Autry. Roy Rogers. Someone had doctored the photos so each star was holding a sashimi plate or bottle of sake in place of a gun or lariat. The only thing missing was a karaoke machine with country-and-western songs.

"You'll simply adore Joe," Lila whispered in my ear. "He's a master with exotic food." Exotic didn't sound promising. But I remembered Connor saying most parties were boring, so I decided to give it a go. Tokyo Joe whipped through some swinging saloon doors with a Japanese sun painted on them.

"Try one of these," he said, offering me a plate full of what looked like tiny red jelly beans wrapped in snake-skin. "I call it Sagebrush Trail sashimi."

I took a bite. A little fishy, but not bad. "What's in it?" I asked warily.

"Octopus. Salmon eggs. Soy barbecue sauce." My face must have gone totally slack. Joe took this as a good sign. He did his best John Wayne impression. "Pilgrim, is that a happy face I see?"

"Isn't it divine?" Lila asked me.

"It's certainly . . . interesting." Note to self: Add "find caterer" to list.

"Here, try this one. It's my specialty of the house. I call it Wyatt Eel." Joe offered something resembling a pig's tongue. Maybe this was the time to mention that no-eel diet I was on. I stared at it, waiting for it to transform into little cucumber sandwiches.

"Oh, for heaven's sake," Lila huffed after a full minute of paralysis on my part. She grabbed the eel thing and took a bite. "It's delicious. You've outdone yourself, Joe. Anyone would be proud to serve this as their cuisine de soiree, even to a bunch of backwoods sixteen-year-olds." Joe beamed with pride, and Lila began discussing the menu and costs right in front of me. A new movie played in my head. Open on NYU review board screening documentary of Sweet Sixteen party. Long shot of confused faces watching Japanese cowboys serving raw fish to grossed-out kids. Hold as review board registers queasy feelings. Cut to board throwing documentary in trash. Fast-forward to Kari selling pencils on street corner.

I needed to stop things before they went too far. I was not my mother. I could stand up to Lila.

"Lila, can we talk?" I said meekly.

"In a minute, Kari Elizabeth. Now, Joe. I'm thinking

a cake shaped like a large salmon would be daring. To stick with the theme."

Salmon cake? This was getting dire. "Maybe we should talk about this . . . ," I suggested.

"But darling, it's perfect. Oh, I love the paper stage-coaches you have in the back room. Could we get some of those?"

I almost groaned out loud. What was next—pin the tail on the sashimi? Lila was out of control.

"How about I loan you my karaoke machine? Kids love it!" Joe clapped in excitement.

"Won-der-ful!" Lila gasped.

Karaoke. The kiss of party death. I had to stop them. Had to seize control.

"I don't want this," I said in a hoarse whisper.

"What?" Lila acted as if I'd stung her.

"I mean, I don't think sushi is such a good idea at a party. There's always the threat of . . ." I couldn't think of what to say to get out of this nightmare. ". . . of food poisoning!"

"My sushi is expertly prepared," Joe said in real earnestness.

"No doubt, Mr. . . . Joe. But you know. Hot night, raw fish? We just can't take the legal risk. I'm sure you understand." I realized I was backing toward the exit. "Thanks

so much for your time. You've got a great place here."

"Wait. I haven't even shown you the karaoke country-and-western bar . . . ," Joe called, but I was already out the door and halfway to the car. Lila came fuming after me. I could almost see smoke coming out of her ears.

"Well, that's the last time I try to be a part of your life," she snapped. It was a total drama-queen moment, but it still made me feel pretty ungrateful.

"Lila . . . ," I began. "I know you want to help. It's just that I want to plan this party. They're *my* friends. Maybe they're not as adventurous as you are, but I know what they like. Can we just smoke the peace pipe?"

Lila was concentrating very hard on the road ahead of us. The Jesus mobile hummed while we rode silently past country lanes and metal mailboxes with PO addresses. She rolled up her window and flicked on the air-conditioning, which only made it feel more humid inside the car.

Finally she spoke, her voice jagged as glass shards. "You have no vision, Kari Elizabeth. Just like your father."

It was supposed to hurt, and it did. I didn't know whether to be angrier that she'd insulted me or Daddy.

In the end I said nothing, just let that tightness in my throat choke back the tears while I counted the horses I saw out my window.

Cut to girl on horseback. The horse rises and falls with her every move. After months of hard work the girl has tamed him. And now she's free to ride as long, as fast, and as far as she likes, tasting the wind all the way.

By that night I had called half a dozen places, looking to rent party space. They were either booked or way too much money. The last place I called suggested holding the party at a roller rink. Images of sixth-grade birthdays flooded over me. Thanks, but no thanks. When I'd crossed the last name off my sad to-do list, I threw it in the trash and tried to come up with a plan B. And a caterer. Oh, and a casting director.

Lila was on a date, and my mom was at a psychic convention, so I was on baby-sitting duty. It was a double curse since Theo's band was practicing in the garage and Isis and her goth friends were listening to rock dirges in her room. I tried to ignore them all and started crafting an intro for my film.

I perched the video cam on a makeshift tripod made from my dresser and a phone book. Running back and forth between my spot on the bed and the director's berth behind the lens, I figured out how to film myself without cropping off the top of my head or anything. The camera rolled. I assumed my best serious journalist look.

"I'm Kari Dobbins." Cut! I was giving the camera a

profile. Not my most flattering angle. Facing forward, I tried again. "Hi. I'm Kari Dobbins. And this is a glimpse into a world few people ever really see in all its glory. The world of a Sweet Sixteen party." The depressed thud from Isis's stereo was beating through my walls, making it hard to think. I tried to continue. "Tonight you'll see how a normal, average teenage girl . . ."

An excruciating sound nearly threw me off the bed. Feedback. Lots of feedback. What followed wasn't much better. A Jimi Hendrix song with a polka beat shook the whole upstairs. At least, I think it was a Jimi Hendrix song.

Isis came out of her room, saw me, then disappeared again like the groundhog after seeing its shadow. I followed her into her room. There were three other black-clad kids sitting on her floor, looking gloomy.

"Did Mom say you could have company?" I shouted over the din.

"We get together every Sunday night. Notice things much?" She had a point. Isis's entire life seemed to take place in a fog. I noticed the kids had our Pictionary game out, which struck me as beyond hilarious.

"I'm getting a headache."

No one moved.

"Turn the music down." It was like I was invisible. I pulled out the big guns. "Now, Rachel."

Isis shot me her most hateful glance but made no move for the volume button.

A kid with shoe-polish black hair took in my polo shirt and khakis. "You must be the sister who has no imagination."

Okay, enough was enough. "No, I'm the sister who's kicking you all out," I retorted. I needed to get some work done.

"You can't do that," Isis snapped.

"Mom left me in charge. It's a school night. You need to be doing school night things. You have five minutes to break up the Gothketeers. I'm going down to deal with Theo."

The basement was a jumble of cables and amps. I was amazed something hadn't caught fire. I had to make a time-out gesture to get the band to quit.

"Excuse me, but this is a closed rehearsal. No fans allowed." Theo's voice broke as he was talking, which undermined the effect he was going for.

"It's not just closed. It's over. Good night, guys. Time to pack up and hit the trail."

A chorus of outrage and disgust erupted. "Dude, are you gonna let some chick tell you what to do?" the bass player demanded of Theo.

The drummer joined in. I recognized his voice from the answering machine. The one who handed out the tardy slips for Ina Goddah Nagilah. "Yeah. You've got as much right to live here as she does!"

Theo was growing bolder by the minute. After a few minutes of goading he'd probably work up to a full "you can't make me," followed by an hour of loud pouting. I stepped in. "Can it, pip-squeak. I'm in charge. I say you're out of here." Taking charge felt good. And once the music geeks and gothsters were safely out of our house, I could work on my project in peace.

The saxophone player was cursing under his breath. "You haven't heard the last of us!"

Upstairs, the doorbell rang. Probably somebody looking for donations. I ran upstairs and threw open the door. "We already gave . . ." My heart zoomed up to my head like one of those bell ringers you hit at a carnival.

"Hi. I thought maybe you could use a study break."

Connor Reese was standing on my front porch, looking around like an actor who'd wandered onto the wrong set. He handed me a pint of cookies and cream, my favorite.

My mouth opened. When no sound came out, I closed it again.

"Can I come in? Or is your grandmother still asleep? If so, you might want to check her breathing."

"Come in," I said. It was almost a whimper.

Connor stood in our foyer and took in the whole weirdo ambiance in one head pivot.

"This is some house," he said.

I cringed. Theo's band members filed past us, nearly upending me in the process. The drummer turned to face me before he left. "This isn't over, sister of Theo. Not by a long shot. We will have *revenge!*" With a sharp pivot he slammed the door behind him. Two seconds later Isis's creepy friends slunk past and out the same door without even looking up.

"Like I said," Connor quipped after a beat. "This is some house."

Connor didn't wait to be invited this time. He wandered through the whole house, taking in the corkboard, the spider art, the mustard walls. I was silently dying a thousand deaths. Especially when Isis cornered him by the upstairs bathroom.

"Are you dating my sister?" She fixed Connor with that unnatural stare of hers.

I practically swallowed my tongue. "Kids say the darnedest things. Isis, I'll help you with your math homework later. Why don't you get ready for bed, okay?"

Isis flipped on the bathroom light. "Because if you are, I think you should know she's a tyrant." She slammed the door in our faces.

"Wow. I think we've just been told off by Morticia," Connor said, winking. He grabbed my hand. "Come on. Let's have some ice cream." God, he was taking this well.

My insides were at war. Knowing that Connor had come all the way over to hand deliver ice cream had me falling even more madly in love. Letting him see the way we lived, warts and all, had me wanting to hide under the bed.

But if Connor felt the urge to run screaming from the Odd Dobbins, he wasn't letting on. Was he so embarrassed for me, he couldn't bring himself to mention it? Whatever. If so, I was grateful. In fact, I was in full-out denial. A nice place to be.

After scooping ice cream into some bowls, we sat on the front porch in Lila's old metal swing from the 1930s.

Connor took a bite and said, "So your mom's working tonight? What does she do?"

"She has a, um, sort of New Age business," I said carefully. "Remember her tarot card readings from Nan's party? That's what she does."

Connor nodded gamely. "Oh yeah. Right."

"What about your mom? What's she do?" I asked so we didn't have to think about my mom for too much longer.

"Corporate lawyer. Makes some nice change. She's really good at it, too."

She sounded like a movie heroine. Cut to Connor's mom in a pin-striped suit, fighting for truth, justice . . . and corporate profits. Well, I'd work on it.

"Funny thing is, my dad's a lawyer, too. Ever try to win an argument against two professional arguers? Don't even try." He laughed, but I sensed a note of sadness there.

The director in me wanted to go deeper. But there was something I wanted to know even more. "So . . . ," I started. I took a bite of ice cream and stared across the street at Mr. Jones's lilac bushes. "Have you . . . talked to Nan lately?"

Connor took my chin in his hand and turned my face toward his. He spoke very clearly. "Nan and I are so over, it's not even funny."

"But you were together for a year. That's a long time. . . ."

"And how many times did we break up during that year?" He dropped his hand. My chin still felt warm from his touch. "Nan's like my mom. She loves a good fight. I'm tired of going so many rounds. I'd just like things to be simple. Easy for a while. You know what I mean?"

Did I ever. A breeze blew my hair into my face, tickling my nose. The streetlights were all on now, and the world was quiet and peaceful. Connor and I rocked on

the swing with its comforting creak. I was dying for him to ask me six little words: Will you go out with me?

"How's the big party plan coming?" Not the six words I was looking for.

"Good, good," I muttered, bouncing my head up and down for reinforcement.

"Good," he said. "Good is . . . good."

I hadn't felt this much tension since Mom took me to buy my first bra. We ate our ice cream in silence. I could hear the scrape-scrape of our spoons against our bowls. I drifted off, letting myself sink into a fantasy where Connor swept me into his arms and covered my neck in kisses.

"Whatcha thinking about?" Connor asked.

I snapped my head around so fast, I nearly hit the swing. *Oh, nothing. Just planning our marriage.* "Uh . . . my friends . . . Dee and Jared," I lied, desperate to cover.

Connor put down his bowl and stretched his arm across the back of the swing. "What about them?"

"Oh, total *YM* stuff. They like each other, and I'm trying to hook them up. Not an easy task, I can tell you."

"Jared's not coming through on the call? But she wants him to?"

Exactly. "Right," I warbled.

"Hmmm, tough break." He pushed us gently, using

only his heels. I swear I could hear my own blood pooling in my ears. I wanted him to ask me out that bad. "Well," he said after what seemed an eternity. "Maybe we should double date."

Oh my God. He said the *D* word! And "we." Now he was waiting for something. What was it? Oh yeah, this was my line! "Yeah. We could do that." Oh, we could soooo do that. I didn't want to come across as a complete spastic. "Actually, I need to check out a restaurant for my party. Maybe we could all go? Next Saturday?" I knew just the place to make an impression, too. Magnolia. The nicest place in town.

"Next Saturday it is. Let's work on the lovebirds."

Yeah, let's, I thought. I was vaguely aware that our heads were getting closer together. I could see his pillowy lips and his impossibly long lashes like an extreme close-up. I hoped I didn't have any ice cream caked around my mouth.

Suddenly a car screeched into my driveway, nearly blinding me with its headlights. The dogs were totally freaked and barked like crazy. Nan Tatum jumped out of the car and ran up to the porch. She had been crying, but she still had that perfect cover girl face. Her arms were crossed, and her head was high. Her voice was shaky, though. "Your mom said you were over here." Nan didn't look in my direction at all.

"What's the matter?" He sounded concerned. People get concerned over other people all the time, right? It didn't necessarily mean he was still under the magic sway of the gorgeous, perfect, impossible, and irresistible Nan Tatum. Did it?

Nan started to cry. That Hollywood kind of crying that makes movie stars look so beautifully doomed. Crying makes my nose run and my eyes swell in a non-movie-star way.

"It's Snuggles. He got out and was hit by a car. The vet says he'll be okay, but . . ." The crying started again.

Okay. This is gonna make me sound really mean, but all I could think was, *She named her dog Snuggles?* The poor creature had probably tried to commit suicide.

Connor picked a leaf off the porch. "I'm sorry, Nan."

Nan stopped crying and glared at Connor. "I can't believe you're being so cold. This is the worst thing that's ever happened to me, and you don't even care. I knew I shouldn't have come." She ran to her car.

Connor called after her, "Wait, Nan!"

My heart sank. Connor gave me a wince and shrug that seemed to say, "What can I do?" "I know it's retarded, but that dog means everything to her," he muttered.

I tried to look mature and noble like Olivia de Havilland in *Gone with the Wind*. It probably just made

me look constipated. "No. I understand. I should probably check on the hellions. It's too quiet in there."

"You're a doll," he said, getting up to leave.

I stood to watch him go. I don't know why. Halfway down the walk Connor turned back and blew me a little kiss that only I could see. Then he was gone, leaving me to float inside.

After Connor's visit, the house didn't seem quite as shabby as before. With a little paint, some killer food, and a great band, I could pull off the party here. I *would* pull off the party here.

Well, technically I had no choice. But that wasn't what I was thinking as I climbed up the stairs in a daze. I was thinking that if Connor Reese could ask me out, there was hope for any and everything.

chapter 7

By Monday morning I was nearly bursting to talk to Dee. We now had a party and a double date to prepare for, and I was getting psyched.

We met at our shared locker between first and second period. We weren't supposed to be sharing a locker. It made teachers nervous, like the combined hormonal flimflam of two high schoolers could turn a locker into a time portal or something. Dee came bounding up as I spun our combination.

"Your note said it was important," Dee said. Her eyes suddenly went wide. "Oh my God. You can't tell I'm wearing a pad, can you?" Dee started trying to see behind herself like a dog chasing its tail.

"Relax. It's good news." I paused for effect. "Guess who's going on a double date Saturday night?"

Dee looked excited but clueless. "Who?"

"We are, dorkus. You, me, Jared. And Connor."

Dee did a silent squeal and squeezed my arm. "No way."

"Way. Very way." I took out the compact Dee kept hidden in the back of the locker and put a swipe of powder on my oily chin. I waited for my reflection to change to suit my happiness. Lank, split-end-infested hair stared back. "We need a Cinderella moment. I can't go out with Connor looking like this."

Dee mustered her best can-do voice. "I could bring over my curling iron and *Cosmo*'s makeup tips for May."

I shook my head. "Let's be real. I'm thinking the splurge route: head-to-toe makeovers at Splendor." Splendor was only the most chichi salon in town.

"Oh, that is too Roswell. I was just thinking the same thing." Dee gave a little jump. I had to love her spirit.

Two seconds later her face went deer in headlights. "He's coming."

I didn't want to turn around and make a big deal out of it. "Which he?"

Jared's voice answered the question. "Hey. What's up?"

"Nothing!" Dee and I yelped in unison. Very suave. Jared gave us the eyebrow.

"Wow. That much nothing, huh?"

"You look nice today, Jared. I really like your earring," Dee blurted out. She dropped her books in front of her pants in what I assumed was an effort to conceal the nonexistent pad problem.

Jared grinned. "Well, thanks, Malloy. See, Karnage. Some people recognize that I am a god among men."

Bull's-eye. With my deft planning I'd be directing a sappy love scene between Jared and Dee by the end of Saturday night.

During the eternity known as last period I passed a rough draft of my party invitation to Dee. It started: *Attention, sophomore class: Be a movie star, or just look like one. Attend this Sweet Sixteen party, and you could be part of a documentary about life, liberty, and being sixteen.*

Dee stuffed it under a chapter on the colonies just as Mr. White, our history teacher, made one of his long swoops through the desk aisles, looking for contraband.

Dee lifted up the chapter and read the note. She scribbled something and, after a quick glance at White, passed it back. She'd added the word *awesome* before *documentary*. So Dee.

Mr. White was preoccupied with writing *taxation without representation* on the board, as if we hadn't absorbed it after three mentions. I threw a paper wad at Dee, and she turned my way.

"*Awesome?*" I mouthed sarcastically.

"Keeps *documentary* from sounding too dire," she whispered.

"Yeah, but . . ."

Mr. White's chalk had stopped.

"Miss Dobbins? Do you have something you'd like

to share with the class?" I tried to shove the paper under my book but missed, and it went sailing onto the floor just as Mr. White bent to pick it up.

Here it came. The sadistic reading aloud thing that adults never seemed to tire of. To my surprise, White registered the info, then handed it back to me with a too easy put-down. "Kari, if you're interested in parties, may I suggest that you read your chapter on the Boston Tea Party this evening. That goes for everyone."

A chorus of groans nearly drowned out the bell. Mr. White stopped me on my way out. "Kari, keep your social life confined to after school."

Still, I had to be grateful to White. His finger waving made me just late enough to bump into Connor coming into the commons. I saw him first and wondered if he'd be all cool the way guys get in public after you've had a private moment together.

Connor looked up, and for a minute I wasn't sure he recognized me. But then the killer smile popped into place, and he gave me a small wave. "Hey. Didn't see you after fourth period today."

Did he know I ran into him accidentally on purpose most days? "That's me. Unpredictable."

"You? Unpredictable? No way. You're steady as a rock."

I winced a little. A girl likes to be thought of as magical.

Fresh. Even tragic but unforgettable in a *Wuthering Heights* way. Like Nan. It was all I could do to keep from asking what had happened last night when he sailed off in her convertible to check on the unfortunate Mr. Snuggles. "Well, I could surprise you," I said with all the coyness I could muster.

"Speaking of surprises . . . how's Operation Lovebird going?"

"Good," I said, trying to shake the predictable quote. "They don't suspect a thing." At least, Jared didn't.

"Where are we going Saturday?"

"To . . ." I stopped. It was time to add an air of mystery. "Someplace . . . surprising."

"Color me intrigued." We had reached Connor's car. "I'd give you a lift, but I've got to pick up my dad."

"No issue," I said. "Got wheels, will travel." The petri dish of high school culture moved all around us.

"Well, see ya." Connor ducked his head into his car and started the ignition.

It was probably too early for a kiss, anyway, I told myself on the way to the Jesus mobile. I'd parked my usual four blocks from school to avoid the gawks that came with our car. If Connor wanted surprises, he'd get one. The makeover was the best idea I'd had yet.

Mom was puttering around when I got home. "You

got some more in the mail today," she said, wafting past me with a pot of very dead begonias. She handed me brochures from various party outfitters—everything from basic chip and dip to full-scale day trips and boat cruises on a lake. What I needed was a sound system, a white tent, great food, and lots of people showing up ready to bare their souls on camera to ensure my place in film school. Mom watered the dead begonias and placed the overflowing brown carcass back on our magazine-encrusted windowsill. Oh yeah. I needed to do something about my family, too.

"So, what can we do to help out with the party?" Mom asked. It caught me off guard.

"Do?" I repeated. "How about nothing? That would be really helpful."

Mom pulled a copy of *Tarot Now* from the magazine stack and tore out an article. "You know, sweetie, maybe if you got everybody involved, they'd feel like it was their party, too."

"Well, it's not." I hadn't meant to sound so harsh. I just wanted this to be mine. A smooth show.

"What I mean is, if everybody has something to take care of, they'll be able to help you make sure the party goes off without a hitch. So delegate a little."

Delegate. Directors had to delegate all the time.

That's why they had crews. But could I really trust Theo and Isis and Lila and even Mom to do anything right?

Mom reached over and fluffed the crackly leaves on the plant, giving me the old I'm-not-looking-at-you-but . . .

The fact is, I *was* a little overwhelmed. And if I gave them explicit instructions, they couldn't mess it up. It would be step one in my revamp of the Dobbins family aura.

"Fine." I sighed. "I'll delegate. God help me." Mom smiled absently and kissed me on the head on her way to the kitchen to start dinner.

My camera was waiting for me like an old friend when I got upstairs. I turned it on and got a great shot of all the brochures splayed out on my bed. "This is just a small assortment of the vast choices today's teenager has when it comes to arranging the perfect Sweet Sixteen."

Yuck. Too CNN. This film stuff was harder than it looked. While I thought of something clever to say, I took a long pan of my room. Sort of an establishing shot. The camera swooped over my carefully stacked CDs, the desk where my blue ballpoints rested in a mason jar, the neatly made bed. It came to rest on my father's picture. I got a far-off look at him through the long lens.

I'm going after it, Daddy. And I'm pulling them all back from their shadow selves while I do.

* * *

"Ohmigod! It's official—you're in print!" Dee screamed at me.

It was Friday morning, and I had gone two whole days without running into Connor. I was so consumed with the does-he-or-doesn't-he question that I didn't even notice that my party invite had made the *Buccaneer Weekly*. I was opening our locker when Dee came running up with a copy.

I looked at the school paper, but all I saw was an ad for wart cream. Then, just above the wart cream, in one of fate's delicious little moments, I saw my invitation: *Attention, sophomore class: Be a movie star, or just look like one. Attend this Sweet Sixteen party, and you could be part of an awesome documentary about life, liberty, and being sixteen.* I had to admit, the *awesome* did help. *Everyone is welcome—preppies, jocks, bandies, drama queens, brains, neopunks, ravers, and anyone else. Saturday, May 12th. 8:00 P.M. till??? Food. Bevies. Music. Maybe even film immortality. RSVP @ kdobbins@innovate.net for directions.*

By lunch the news had hit Greenway High like a monsoon. Swarms of kids I'd never even laid eyes on were tracking me from class to class to ask about the party. Some guy in a striped shirt crashed my gym class to audition with his ukulele version of "The Itsy Bitsy Spider."

It approached stalkersville at times, but the attention

felt amazing. People were looking at me like a serious person rather than a sideshow refugee. I was looking forward to showing them and myself what I could do with a camera and an idea.

A group of preppies cornered me in study hall to ask questions. "Where's the party going to be?" a perky pep squader asked.

"My house," I answered.

"Oh." She seemed disappointed and started to walk away.

"We're having a sound system put in," I added. "And we're setting up several rooms as interview areas." She was practically drooling, and I wasn't even totally lying, either. It was Theo's job to find the sound system. All part of my delegate-and-conquer routine. I made a mental note to ride him about it later.

In study hall a few of the drama-ramas sneaked over to get the goods. Dave Kimball, the school's best (hammiest) actor, stretched out next to me. "I hear this tape could be seen by some very influential people." Dave Kimball had once referred to my family as "those weirdos," so I couldn't resist having a little fun with him.

"Yeah," I said in my best offhand tone. "There might be some heavy hitters there." Me. Jared. Dee. Fric and Frac. "But I don't want it to get around. You know how it is."

Dave wasn't about to let on that he didn't know. He

gave me a thumbs-up, then reached into his backpack and pulled out a head shot from his theater camp in Atlanta. A big, goofy picture of Dave holding a skull in a serious pose stared back at me.

I tried to keep a straight face. "Thanks, Dave. I'll keep this on file."

Sixth period was a free one for me. That's when I caught up with Dee and Jared in the library. Jared was always in the library, drawing. Dee had cut gym to follow him. Yowza.

She was pretending to read *The Scarlet Letter,* but I could see she was really mooning over Jared. Jared closed his notebook the minute I came by the table. More secrets.

"Hi," I whispered, much to the annoyance of our school librarian, Mrs. Wolf.

"Well, if it isn't the director herself. Or is that directress? I never know."

"I guess this party is getting some pretty outrageous press around school," I admitted.

"You would not believe how much people are talking about it," Dee said. She gave me an imploring look and mouthed, "Say something."

The date. Time to play matchmaker. "Yo, Jar."

"Yes, O Hitchcock of Greenway High."

"I kinda need a favor."

Jared's head popped up from his notebook.

"It's for the party. I want you to go with me and Dee to Magnolia on tomorrow. I'm checking out their menu for the party." Something told me not to mention Connor. Either Jared would be scared off at the date possibility, or he'd make fun of me for asking Connor out.

Jared made a whistling noise. Mrs. Wolf threw us a threatening glance. Jared lowered his voice. "Kinda pricey there, isn't it?"

I had exactly five hundred dollars to spend on everything from food to my dress. I'd have to make it stretch. "That's my problem. Are you coming or not?"

"Free meal? Count me in."

I stole a glance at Dee, who was beaming.

"Don't look now," Jared said quietly, "but here comes another curious bunch."

A guy and two girls were heading our way. I'd seen them at Café Vortex with Connor. They were bandies and heavily into the swing scene. The guy nodded at me. "Hey."

"Hey," I said back.

"I'm Scott. This is Charlotte and Cheryl." The girls smiled and said hi. "Who's doing the music for this shindig? You got a band lined up?"

I had to admit I didn't. I was leaning toward a DJ.

But if I told Scott that, he'd probably talk me into hiring his band, if he had a band, which I had a sneaking feeling he did.

"A band," I repeated. "Well, I . . ."

"She's having Robin's Hoods!" Dee blurted out.

"Shhhhhh!" Mrs. Wolf hissed.

Dee lowered her voice. "Have you ever heard them? They're awesome!"

My jaw nearly hit the table.

"Chicklet, I'm the biggest Robin's Hoods fan around," Scott said, looking pretty overjoyed. "Dig it. We'll be there. And we'll spread the word."

"No! Don't do that. . . ." I trailed off as the three swingers bopped off to parts unknown.

I punched Dee on the arm. "How could you say that?"

"I couldn't help it. I just wanted them to think your party was gonna be the best. I'm sorry."

"Great. Well, maybe they won't tell anybody else." My heart stopped as I saw Connor striding up to our table. He pulled a chair over to me.

"Hey! I hear you're having Robin's Hoods play your party. That is the coolest. Way to go!" He bumped me with his chair in a completely adorable way, and I knew instantly I'd commit high crimes to secure Robin's Hoods for my party.

Jared rolled his eyes and stood up.

"Are you leaving?" Dee asked, a little desperately. She looked at me, then at Connor, then back at me. "Do you need a ride?"

Jared seemed to think it over. I held my breath. "Yeah. Great. Thanks, Malloy."

They walked through the library's swinging double doors, looking like a pair of novelty salt-and-pepper shakers. Odd but somehow well matched.

"Come on. I'll walk you," Connor said after the three-thirty bell rang. We strolled into the crowded hallway. Kids rushed past us on both sides. One of the cheerleaders marched up to Connor.

"Hi, Connor. Did Nan leave my new scarf at your house last night?"

Connor looked down at his feet. I felt new fear grip my chest. Nan had been at his house last night? I waited for him to say it wasn't true. "No, she didn't."

"Well, if you find it, I need it back."

The fear spread out from my chest like rivers from an icy delta. I forced a cool tone into my voice. "So. Nan came by?" I asked, keeping my eyes straight ahead.

Connor stopped and hugged his books in front of him for a minute. "Yeah. She's still upset about her dog."

"Oh. Is he okay?" I didn't care about her stupid dog.

I know that's not a nice thing to say, but I was dissolving inside.

"Look, she came over for, like, twenty minutes. We talked. She left. End of story."

End of story? I was about to have a massive coronary. I needed every misery-inducing detail.

A short guy with thick glasses grabbed my sleeve. "I heard about the pay-per-view deal. Way to go!" I didn't register it. All I could do was picture Nan, beautiful, movie-star Nan, sitting with her head on Connor's shoulder.

"Kari?" Connor pulled me toward him. "Hey. That's all. I promise." He leveled his green-gray eyes at me. Down the hall a group of kids was chattering and pointing at me. I vaguely heard the words *party* and *documentary* bandied about.

"Okay. Sure," I said, but my insides were as jumbled as my mom's sock drawer. I cocked my head toward the curious throng in the hallway. "I better make a quick getaway."

"Sure thing, doll. I'll catch you later." And he was gone.

I ducked down a side hall and into the girls' bathroom, hoping to hide out until the crowd had thinned. My eyes felt tight and watery. Some girls were giggling in the stalls when I came in, so I kept it together.

The door to one of the stalls clanged open, and Nan emerged. Jen came out of the other one.

Great. Just what I needed. I immediately preoccupied myself with an all-consuming hand wash.

Jen stood by the door. Nan didn't budge from her perch by the paper towels. The thump-thumping of my heart told me I was going to have to face her or leave with wet hands. Next thing I knew, Nan was handing me a paper towel.

"Thanks," I said.

"You're welcome, Kari." She'd finally gotten my name right. "Hey, I was just wondering. What were you and Connor doing together the other night?"

"Talking." I shrugged, hoping my voice didn't sound as freaked out as I really was. I unzipped my purse and fiddled around inside it, pretending to look for my keys.

"Really. 'Cause somebody told me that you and Connor went dancing the other night." Nan put on a fresh coat of lipstick in the mirror, then blotted her lips on a paper towel. Her mouth left a perfect *O*.

I felt her watching me, but I didn't answer. A fluorescent light hummed overhead. Nan pulled out a tube of mascara and pumped the wand back and forth in the tube, then continued. "I told them that couldn't be true. That Connor would never go for somebody like you."

"Maybe he wants to branch out," I said, struggling to sound Clint Eastwood cool.

Nan's gaze met mine in the mirror. For a second her expression betrayed anger. Then a slow, beauty-queen smile spread across her face. "Listen, Kari, I'm not trying to be mean or anything. I just don't want you to get hurt. Connor and I really talked last night, and I think he wants to get back together. I wouldn't get too involved with him if I were you."

A heavy weight sat on my chest. I wondered if she was telling me the truth. If she was, then why was she even talking to me? She was lying. Had to be. She needed the 411 on Connor and me as badly as I wanted it on her. A sunbeam cut through the bathroom windowpane, washing everything in a warm haze. "You're not me," I said, feeling bolder. "So don't worry about it."

Nan grabbed her purse. "Okay. But don't say I didn't warn you."

"Yeah, you really should watch it," Jen sneered.

Nan pushed through the bathroom door. Jen followed, then stuck her head back in.

"I hope this doesn't affect my role in your movie," she said before shutting the door.

chapter 8

"Oh my God. You had a close encounter of the Nan kind," Dee said as we made our way to Salon Splendor for our makeovers. The day of the big date was upon us. "Were you afraid she'd, like, start a catfight?"

"Be real, Dee. That only happens in Mariah Carey videos."

"I would've been so freaked. She's just so pretty, you know?"

I didn't need that. "Well, gee, maybe I won't frighten schoolchildren after today's session."

"Oh, Kar, I didn't mean anything. You look great." Looking great wasn't the same thing as being pretty. No way around it.

"Let's just get this show on the road, 'kay?" I said stiffly.

By eleven-thirty Dee and I were sitting in plush leather chairs. Shawnda, our style consultant, recommended a trim and blond highlights for Dee. I decided to take the plunge and cut long layers into my boring shoulder-length bob plus pump up the blond. We changed into big, white bathrobes. Then Shawnda led us into a little room with a dipping pond and incense and sat us in front of the Hubble Telescope of makeup mirrors, which magnified everything on our faces to fun house proportions.

"I'll be back in a sec," Shawnda said, leaving Dee and me alone to examine every nook, cranny, and blemish.

"Oh my God," Dee said. "Why didn't you tell me I had so many blackheads! My chin looks like pepper mill turkey. Eewwww!"

I couldn't get over my nose. In the mirror it seemed to take over, like a giant alien nose ship had landed smack in the middle of my face. "I can't let them cut my hair. Then I'll be nothing but a pair of walking nostrils."

"I thought this was supposed to make us feel better about ourselves, not worse," Dee pointed out.

"Yeah. Ignorance is definitely bliss." I spotted a troubling crater below my bottom lip. "Is that a freckle, or am I starting to sprout hair on my chin like my grandmother?"

"Lila has hair on her chin?"

"She plucks them every morning. She's got a new boyfriend, by the way. This one's a former traveling magician, current weirdo."

"Man, oh, man. Your grandmother and her boyfriends. How do you deal?"

I shrugged. "Ignore them, mostly. My mom always

goes out of her way to make them all seem like part of the family. Inviting them to dinner and stuff."

Dee turned her attention to her eyebrows. "How come your mom doesn't just tell your grandmother to act her age?"

"My mom stand up to Lila? Please. There's a better chance I'll grow up to be a supermodel."

"How do people get to be supermodels, anyway?"

"Grow ten feet and major cheekbones overnight. Who cares." The conversation was starting to make me irritable. For today I wanted to concentrate on making myself wonderful, or as close to wonderful as I could get, and that meant leaving every thought of my family behind.

Dee laughed. "Oh my gosh. I can just see the first time Connor comes over for Sunday night dinner. Lila will probably have some geriatric Siegfried and Roy act over. Your mom will be looking for astral clues in the spaghetti sauce. Isis will probably take dinner in her coffin. And Theo. Well, Theo's Theo—what can I say?"

"They're not that bad," I said a little defensively, but I knew she was right. Maybe I had gotten them to do a few things on my to-do list, but it wasn't the same as changing them.

Dee kept laughing. "Oh yes, they are, Kar. I'm totally understating the problem, and you know it." I knew it

wasn't Dee's fault for pointing out the obvious, but I was mad at her, anyway. Wearing a look of concern, I examined a spot at the back of Dee's head. "Are you losing hair back here?"

She freaked. "Oh my God! Oh my God! I'm going bald!"

Okay. It was such a *Melrose* thing to do, but I couldn't seem to stop myself. Every time I dreamed of my perfect life with Connor Reese at my side, I ran smack into the reality that I was raised by circus freaks. I was enjoying my new status as nonweirdo. It felt so right to finally be taken seriously. I liked it, and I wanted more. I was ready to completely make my life over. I was even getting new hair. I could make over my family, too, just like I'd promised Jared I would. I'd be like Henry Higgins in *My Fair Lady*.

"The rain in Spain stays mainly in the plains," I said dreamily.

"What?" Dee asked. I hadn't meant to say it out loud.

"Nothing," I said. Where was Shawnda, our fearless "style consultant," anyway?

As if reading my mind, Shawnda waltzed through the door and led us to the "rinsing station," where we were given a "botanical conditioning experience that actually strengthens your hair every time you shower." The miracle potion was for sale at only twelve ninety-eight plus tax per bottle. Ouch. I'd be doing the Suave conditioning experience instead.

After our hair was conditioned and wrapped in warm towels, we were treated to a neck massage (bliss to the tenth power), pedicure-manicure (Passion Fruit Pink for Dee, Taupe of New York for me), color typing (figures I'm winter . . . the drab months), cut and color, and makeup lessons.

Dee asked the makeup artist how to make her lips look pouty like a model's on a *Cosmo* cover. I didn't get a chance to ask. Miss Lip Liner took one look at me and said sympathetically, "And I can show you how to make your nose look a little less . . . a little more . . . with the right shading you'll hardly notice it at all."

Hi. Just sign me up for the ego-shrinkage treatment. As I sulked, the makeup guru blended a little brown shadow on the sides of my nose. When she was satisfied, she stood back and shoved a small mirror into my hand. I was almost afraid to look, but curiosity won in the end. I couldn't believe it. My nose hadn't shrunk to cheerleader size, but it did look better. Less noticeable.

All that was left was for Dee and me to sit under some heat lamps to set our highlights. I took this as my opportunity to coach Dee a little on Jared. Sure, they'd

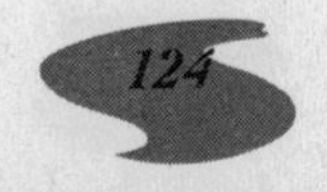

been friends for years. But everything was different now. We needed new direction.

"Okay," I began. "What's your favorite movie of all time?"

"Definitely *Titanic*!" Dee gushed.

Clearly I had my work cut out for me. "Annnh! No, but thank you for playing. Pick another movie."

"But I saw *Titanic* eight times. I would've gone again, but my mom staged an intervention with my allowance."

"Good for her. Dee, you can't pick *Titanic*. It's so . . . I don't know . . . generic."

"Well, maybe I am generic. I mean, we don't all have to be superheroes, do we?"

Dee was selling herself short again. I refused to let her drag her insecurity blanket around. "Dee," I said sweetly but as firmly as possible. "Do you want to date Jared or not?"

"Yes. I mean, I think so. He is sort of babe-o-matic. And have you noticed how his body's filling out?"

"He's a hottie in training, the alt-rock Ken doll. So, are you prepared to be Barbie, or do you just want to be Francie or Skipper your whole life?"

"At least I'm not Midge."

"Heaven forbid. Look, you don't have to give up *Titanic*. But get familiar with Jared's faves. Like the Marx Brothers."

"I've never seen one of their movies."

"Rent one. That's your homework for this weekend."

"I hate homework."

"No pain, no gain. Midge," I said pointedly.

"Oh, all right." Dee sighed. She picked up a copy of *Teen* and started to look up her horoscope. I took the magazine out of her hands and threw it on the floor.

"And another thing—Jared would never take any girl seriously who read *Teen* out in the open. Start reading what he reads: comic books. *Sci-Fi Quarterly. Spin.* Speaking of *Spin,* let's talk music. Jared's fave bands are Cake and Oasis. He practically worships the Chemical Brothers."

"You know I listen to Mariah Carey." Dee was starting to whine. Not a good sign.

"Survey says: Whining is least attractive trait to opposite sex."

"It just seems like I'm trying to be somebody else."

I took a deep breath and thought about how to answer her. "It's not that. Really. It's just you like him; he likes you. We're just coming up with things to talk about. That's all."

"Well, why can't Jared go rent *Titanic,* then?"

Because life is unfair. Because everything worth having takes work. Because Jared wouldn't watch *Titanic* if somebody held him at gunpoint. "Because guys take a

little drawing out." I instantly thought of Connor. How would I draw him out? "It sucks, but there you go."

Dee stuck her long legs out in front of her and admired her frosty pink toes. "I'm just so nervous about tonight."

That made two of us. I tried to imagine Connor and Jared fretting over what to wear and how to keep the conversation going. When I was a director, I was going to make a movie in which guys had to fall all over themselves to get ready for a date.

Dee sat up, panicked. "What do I say to break the ice?"

"Jared likes a smart-ass. He's big on arguing. Just dish it out to him in heaps."

"But I'm not as quick as you are, Kar. What if I just sound stupid?"

"You won't sound stupid, okay? Remember, this is Jared. Jared I-wore-Sears-jeans-till-the-ninth-grade Jameson."

Dee stared up at the ceiling. Her face broke out in a flirty smile. "Yeah. But everything feels different now." She looked over at me. "Okay. Gimme your best shot."

This was good. "Way to go. Now. Pretend I'm Jared and . . ."

"Wait—then who am I?"

I blinked a few times, then spoke slowly. "You're you."

"Right." Dee smiled. "Go on."

I shook it off. "It's B lunch, and we're hanging out

on the commons, waiting for the siren of doom to call us back to fourth period. I say, 'Nice streaks, Malloy. Did you pay someone for those, or is it a medical experiment gone horribly wrong?' And you say . . . ?"

"And I say . . . I say . . ." Dee struggled, then answered triumphantly, "I paid for them."

She looked at me, waiting for the girlfriend seal of approval. The clock ticked on the wall. Cars honked on the street outside. I finally managed to close my open mouth and recover. Apparently Dee wasn't great under date pressure.

"O-kay, that would be one answer. How about, 'They're called highlights, Jameson. Something your life would be missing right about now.' "

"Oooh, good one. But Kaaaar. I can't do that."

"Hello. Whine factor. Rising."

Dee gave me a playful shove on the arm. At least she was coming out of her pout spiral. "All right. Let's try another one."

"Good girl," I said. I thought for a minute. "You're talking about the X-Men, and Jared says, 'The problem with Wolverine is he's two-dimensional. Storm is a much more interesting character.' " I looked at her meaningfully. The strain was making her pupils dilate. "Dee, it's not an AP exam."

"I know. I just want to get it right. I would say, 'I hate that stupid show, and I don't even think Mulder is all that good-looking.'" The pout was coming back.

"Important safety tip? We're talking about *X-Men,* the comic book, not *X-Files,* the show."

"Well, excuse me for living." Dee blew out her breath. "I didn't know there was going to be a pop quiz."

No one knows when there's going to be a pop quiz—that's why it's a "pop"—but I could see Dee was in no mood to have this small fact pointed out. She was getting discouraged. Not what I had intended. I gave her my best pep talk face.

"Look, don't worry about it. Just do your best, okay? I'll guide you through."

Thirty minutes later the bathrobes came off and Dee and I got a glimpse of our new selves in full makeover heaven. I reached up to touch my new layered hairdo. Letting go of all that stringy hair was one of the best decisions of my life. The Kari staring back at me from the mirror had a headful of blond, tousled locks, and she was actually sort of pretty—almost babelike. I couldn't wait to see Connor's reaction. Predictable? I don't think so.

"Hi. What's up?" Jared's mall friend, Mark, was calling to me. He was dropping off some leaflets on the table where the free newspapers and ads for tap-dancing

lessons usually lived. "It's Kari, right?" Why was it that no one seemed sure of my name?

"Hi, Mark. What's up?"

"Just dropping off some ads for my parents' print shop. Did you just get your hair done?"

"Actually, I was donating a kidney in the back room there." He looked a little scared. "Just kidding. Yep. Did the hair thing."

"Looks nice," he said, but he was looking over my shoulder at Dee, the new goddess of Greenway. Dee was working her I'm-too-shy-to-really-look-you-in-the-face look, which she perfected through years of watching Princess Di on TV.

I sighed at the drama of it all. "Dee, Mark. Mark, this is Dee."

There was an exchange of too cute hi's that made me want to run for cover. Then Mark totally freaked me out. "Are you dating Jared?" he asked.

Dee shot me a worried glance.

"No," I said. "Why?"

"Nothing. Just wondered, that's all. So, you're not his girlfriend?"

A creepy feeling made its way up my neck. Was Mark hitting on me? Was that what the whole rush-out-of-the-mall vibe had been about last week with

Jared? "I'm not his girlfriend," I said very emphatically. Then I realized I'd left myself open. He'd probably ask me to don Spock ears and accompany him to a Trekkie convention. "I'm sort of seeing somebody," I added.

"Oh," Mark said. If he was crushed, he didn't act it. "Well, have a good one. Don't do anything I wouldn't do."

Dee laughed, and I pulled her out of the salon behind me. I was tired of being a professional nongirlfriend. Tonight would be my night. Lights. Camera. Time for serious action.

I made my entrance down the stairs, wearing a blue Chinese-inspired shift. It was a little more formfitting than I was used to, and I kept smoothing it down with every step. Theo fell on the floor in a combo fake rhapsody–borderline seizure. "Oooooh, she's so girly! I may die!"

"I should be so lucky," I snarled.

Isis looked up from her book for a millisecond, then resumed reading. Nothing like a vote of confidence.

"Honey, you look wonderful," Mom said, clasping her hands in front of her. She had painted some stars and moons on them. There was a whole Milky Way happening on the backs of her long fingers. I resisted the irritated urge to scrub them clean.

"It needs something," Lila murmured, looking me up and down like a side table in an antiques shop. "I have just the thing." With Hefty perched on her shoulder, she marched upstairs. I didn't even want to know what she was getting me.

"So I look okay?" I was fishing big time.

Theo was making Silly Putty sculptures of his favorite rock stars. He was putting them in little frames to hang on the wall. "Yeah. If it weren't for your schnoz, you'd be almost pretty."

"So not helping," I said. I'd be hiding those frames later.

Isis looked up from her book again. "Did you talk to that casting director?"

"What casting director?"

"That one who called you back yesterday. Some lady."

Why couldn't anybody leave a message like normal people do? "Isis, what did she say?"

"To call her back by five before she made up her schedule and went on vacation."

My heart dropped into my stomach like a free-falling elevator. "*What?* How could you forget to tell me that?"

Isis got a skittish kitten look, then recovered. "Guess you were too busy getting beautiful."

"Could you be a little more useless next time?" I

barked. It wasn't the nicest thing I could have said, but I was seriously annoyed. A casting director would have been a huge coup. She might have even been able to write me a letter of recommendation when the time came, as a witness to the film process.

"I'm sure she'll come if you call her," Mom said in that peace-and-harmony way.

"It doesn't work that way, Mom. This is the real world."

Mom got a pinched look, and I felt bad for snapping.

Lila descended on me, holding up a necklace. At least, I think it was a necklace. It was huge, with glycerin-encased beetles and ladybugs hanging from it clothesline style. "I got this in Cairo twenty years ago. You can bet no one else will be wearing one of these."

No kidding. I stood paralyzed as Lila fitted the clasp behind me. "Won-der-ful!" she sang.

My watch read seven-thirty. It was too early to leave, but I couldn't take another minute of this B horror movie called my family. As soon as I got in the car, I threw off the necklace and shoved it into my glove compartment. Then I made my way toward the fiery sunset and the restaurant, praying the evening would improve drastically.

chapter 9

I was the first person at Magnolia. It gave me a chance to decompress and get into the right mood. The place was beyond gorgeous. There were oak-paneled walls and Chinese vases filled with expensive floral arrangements. Peeking into the main dining room, I could see crisp, white tablecloths and antique lamps giving off romantic mood lighting at each table. It was going to be so perfect.

My shooting script was flowing smoothly in my head. It went something like this: Major hottie struck dumb by new girlfriend's beauteous makeover, pledges eternal love oath over second course. Girlfriend's two dearest friends discover tender romance over dessert. This was what being a director was like. Calling the shots. Arranging the scene till it was flawless. Then sitting back and watching it play.

Dee was the next person through the door. Her figure looked even more spectacular than usual in her short teal silk dress. I felt a minute of panic, wondering if Connor would take one look at Dee and forget all about me.

Dee, as usual, said the right thing. "Ohmigod, you are so beautiful! I love your new hair—very bouncin' and behavin'."

"You don't think I used too much hair spray, do you?"

"No way. Connor's gonna flip out." She checked her makeup with a small compact mirror. "I'm a little nervous about Jared. Suppose he doesn't think of me *that way?*"

"You'll be fine," I said, stealing a quick look at her for lipstick on the teeth. "Just remember everything we went over."

We didn't have too long to agonize. Jared and Connor walked in together. The sight of Connor in a vintage cream-colored suit with a silver tie almost knocked me over. Jared looked grumpy and uncomfortable in his wrinkled seersucker suit, which was a little too short on him. He had loosened his tie already. His hair was in its usual long, unruly state.

Connor smiled at me and kissed my hand. I wanted to freeze-frame that moment forever. I wanted it etched onto the backs of my eyelids so every blink brought the moment back.

"Wow." Connor whistled appreciatively. "You sure do clean up nice, Miss Dobbins."

Jared had a bad-smell face. "What's with the poofy hair?"

"It's my new 'do." I bristled. "Very chic."

"If you're fifty and on your fourth husband, I guess."

Jared was clearly ticked off at me. Now that he'd seen Connor, he probably realized he'd been set up. Oh, well. He'd get over it soon enough. Jared took a look around. "So this is the famous Magnolia. . . ."

"Jared," I said through clenched teeth. "You haven't said hi to Dee yet."

Dee lit up like a birthday party. Jared registered the gorgeousity package. Whew. "Hey, Dee."

"Hey, Jared."

Connor nudged me slightly in the ribs. It was quiet. Jared seemed completely tongue-tied. I was silently begging Jared to say something sweet and romantic.

What was I thinking?

Jared looked around nervously. "So what's a guy have to do to get some service around here?"

A wave of embarrassment washed over me. Connor showed off his trademark calm by walking up to the maitre d' and announcing our arrival, party of four. The maitre d' said hello to Connor like they were old friends, and Connor called him Frank. I couldn't help being impressed. Frank showed us to a table tucked away in an alcove and handed us menus.

My menu swung open, and I about died. The cheapest item was roasted game hen, and it was twenty-six

ninety-five. I wasn't even sure I liked roasted game hen, but for twenty-six ninety-five, I wasn't going to find out. I mean, I knew the place would be expensive, but I didn't imagine it would be more than a hundred dollars for the four of us. I did some quick calculations in my head. If I ordered a six-dollar salad and a nine ninety-five appetizer, then skipped dessert, I'd hopefully have enough to cover Connor and me. I prayed Dee had enough for her part. One thing was for sure, Magnolia was out of the question for a catering choice. A second sour note in my evening.

Jared took a sip of water and sputtered as he opened his menu. "Holy inflation, Batman! Isn't this joint a little ritzy to cater your party, Karnage?"

"They have a different menu for that," I said icily, then changed the subject. "Doesn't Dee look amazing tonight?"

Jared was buttering a piece of bread in an oblivious state. He looked embarrassed. "She looks like Dee," he said. I could have kicked him. "I like the dress," he added, passing the bread basket to Dee.

Dee gave a little giggle. "I can't eat that. Bread makes you fat."

"Only if you eat a whole loaf of it in one sitting," Jared snarled. "Why do girls get so freaked about weight?"

"I know what you mean," Connor said. They were hitting it off, connecting on that basic guy level.

Dee's cheeks were red and not from her new blush. "Oh yeah? By the way, Jameson, I paid for these streaks. They're called highlights. Not that you've ever had any!" She plopped a piece of bread in her mouth and chewed it with a satisfied smile. Jared and Connor were totally confused.

"O-kay." Jared shook his head. Somebody needed to recover the conversation fumble.

I took a breath. "You know, Dee and I were talking about movies the other day. . . ."

Dee barged in. "I'd rather watch the Marx Brothers any day." She snorted through another mouthful of bread. She was taking Jared's bread statement a little too seriously.

"I love the Marx Brothers," Jared said. Okay, back in the safety zone.

"Me too," Connor chimed in.

"Then it's agreed. We all love the Marx Brothers. Hey, we should rent some of their flicks and hang out at my, um, Dee's house sometime. I'll make popcorn."

Connor gave me a wink. "Sounds great."

Dee was still on another conversation track. "I mean, that whole thing about the workers in Russia fighting for their rights and stuff. The only thing I couldn't figure out was how come if the Marx Brothers were members

of the social party, they didn't have more fun? I don't know. Weird."

I can't even tell you how long the silence lasted. It seemed like a millennium.

Finally Connor spoke up. "I'm sorry. I'm a little out of it. I thought we were talking about the Marx Brothers."

"We are," Dee answered, very proud of herself. "Well, Karl Marx, anyway. I don't know his brothers, but I'm sure they all feel the same way he does because, like, they're family, right?"

Connor put his napkin up to his mouth and started coughing to cover his laugh. His shoulders were still shaking, though.

Jared was staring at Dee with a look that was either wonder (good) or disgust (beyond bad). "Where did you come from, Dee?" he asked.

"I was born right here in Greenway."

Jared laughed. "I was more asking what planet you're originally from. Because you have to be an alien."

Dee threw her napkin on the table and laid down what was a major insult for her. "I know you are, but what am I?" Then she stuck out her tongue. I am not kidding. She actually stuck out her tongue, copping 'tude like I hadn't seen since pre-K.

It was horrible. Dee had turned into one of those

talking robots that suddenly short-circuits, jumbling up all its phrases. And I was the doomed scientist, helpless to do anything to stop my wayward creation.

"Dee," I said quickly. "Could you come with me for a sec? We'll be right back." Smiling, I took Dee's arm and led her to the ladies' room. Even the Magnolia bathrooms were fancy. Ceramic bowls of homemade peach potpourri sat beside the marble sink. "Dee, what movie did you rent?"

Dee was nervously running a comb through her hair. "I don't know. Something about revolution. I asked the guy at the counter if he had anything on Marx, and he pointed me to the history section."

"You rented a movie on Karl Marx, the father of communism, not the Marx Brothers, the comedians!"

"I thought it was weird that it wasn't very funny, but . . ." The true awfulness registered on Dee's face. "Ohmigod. I can't go back out there. He thinks I'm an idiot! Tell Jared that I got sick or something. I have to go home!"

I sat Dee in a chair and calmed her down the way I'd heard about directors calming drama-queen actresses. "Look, it's not that big a deal, okay? In fact, it totally broke the ice. Someday we'll look back on this and all laugh." That someday was going to be a very long time from now.

Dee managed a weak smile and nodded. "Now, let's

go back out there and have a great time," I added.

"Okay." Dee sighed. "But I'm not saying much."

"Fine. I'll do most of the talking till you get your second wind." Dee started for the door. "By the way, you should go ahead and give me your money for you and Jared so I can make it seem like it was all my idea." Dee's face fell, and a hand of fear clawed at my insides. "You did bring cash, didn't you?"

"You didn't tell me to bring money, Kar. I thought you were paying for it."

My legs went wobbly for a second. How was I going to pay for everything? The only person I knew with any money was Lila, and she'd never let me hear the end of it.

The waiter came to take our order. Connor and Jared went for broke—appetizers, entrées, side dishes. I ordered a dinner salad. Dee claimed all that bread had made her sick and didn't ask for a thing. She kept eating the bread, though. By the time dessert rolled around, my stomach was making grumbling noises loud as thunder.

"Man, this chocolate mousse pie is outrageous," Jared said, passing a forkful under my nose. "You sure you don't want a bite?"

My mouth was watering at the thought. "No thanks," I said. I was desperately trying to think of a way to pay for the meal. Did restaurants really make people

wash dishes when they couldn't cough up the cash?

The waiter brought the check on a little tray. My palms were wet. Jared snickered. "Moment of truth, Dobbins."

The waiter's eyes flickered at the Dobbins mention. "Dobbins. Not Henry Dobbins's daughter?"

"Yes," I said softly.

"Then you must be Lila Huntington's granddaughter."

Wariness crept up and took a seat. I nodded.

The waiter shook his head with a look of disbelief I'd come to recognize whenever my family's name was mentioned. "I'll never forget the time she staged a protest on our front lawn. We were serving Maine lobster, as I recall, and she complained that lobsters mate for life. So she painted her body red and performed a dance piece called . . . oh, what was it called? . . . Meditation on a Lobster Boiled to Death. Something like that. And now that I remember, your mother played a triangle while your grandmother danced. They gathered quite a crowd."

I wanted to sink right through the oriental carpet. There were so many horrible Dobbins stories, I'd forgotten half of them.

"She actually did that?" Connor was agape.

"Magnolia was indebted to her. We sold a lot of lobster that night. Well, I hope your meal was enjoyable. Here you are."

"Thank you," I choked out, staring miserably at the check. I let it sit there, untouched, till Jared swiped it and let out a whistle.

"Wow. One hundred and thirty-two smackers and change. And that's without the tip." With a flourish he handed the bill to me. I started looking through my purse on automatic pilot. Kind of like looking in the fridge for something to eat when you've already checked it five times and found nothing there.

Connor took my purse and put it on the floor. "That's pretty stiff. What do you say you let me pay for this?"

"Great!" Dee said cheerily.

I was too stunned to speak.

"Really," Connor said. "My parents have a tab here. They won't mind."

His family had a tab. Mine had a reputation. I burned with the shame of it.

"Besides, I owe you for the ride to Robin's Hoods the other night." Connor went up to the maitre d'.

I tried to breathe normally again. Talk about close calls. I felt like my dad was watching out for me at that moment. It may sound stupid, but that's how I felt.

Jared was mumbling under his breath in a mimicking voice. "His parents have a tab here. Oooh." But I was so relieved, I didn't even care.

Things might have been bumpier than I expected, but I didn't want the night to end yet. I suggested we take a drive.

"Great," Jared said, and he and Dee piled into the back of Connor's car.

"Didn't you bring your car?" I asked Jared.

"Still in the shop," he answered matter-of-factly. Whatever hopes I had for quiet romance would have to wait. It looked like our double date was still on.

"Great locale, Dobbins," Connor said, looking across the large pond at the big, shady trees stretching their fingers across the moonlit sky.

It was my secret hiding place. The old swimming hole near the railroad tracks was what my dad used to call "an oasis in the industrialized desert." My dad wasn't big on developers building on Greenway's lush land. Being so close to the tracks, this place had remained untouched. Jared and Dee had come with me before, but I was excited to share my secret with Connor.

I sat on a big rock by the water. "So glad you approve."

"I've got a great idea!" Dee chirped. "Let's play truth or dare."

"You cannot be serious." Jared groaned. He was skipping pebbles across the smooth surface of the pond, sending

ripples out to the banks. "That is so sixth grade, Dee."

Actually, it was a brilliant idea. That way I could download some crucial info on Connor without coming off as a nagging detective. It would all be part of a game. "I think it's a great idea. Dee, you start."

Dee plopped down next to me on the rock. "Kari, truth or dare?"

I decided to play it relatively safe. "Truth," I said.

"Okay, how many guys have you kissed?"

The truth was, I fit that bad stereotype "Sweet Sixteen and never been kissed." But saying so made me sound like a loser or a prude. Lying was sort of a bad thing in truth or dare, but I saw my loophole. She hadn't said "passionately kissed." It could be any guy, like Theo or my dad. "Two," I said cryptically, and turned to Connor. "Truth or dare."

"Truth."

Where to start? "Connor, where do you want to go to school?"

"I don't know. The 'rents want me to go to law school. But I can't really see helping people with their wills and divorces for the rest of my life."

"You could be a criminal lawyer," I offered. "Save people's lives. Fight for justice. There's a noble cause."

"I don't know. I'm not sure what I want to do. I'll figure it out later. Dee, truth or dare?"

I stared at him for another moment. It bugged me that Connor wasn't committed to a career choice. I don't know why. Maybe because my question fell flat. Or maybe because I'd lived my whole life with a sense of purpose, an overpowering, totally consuming dream. My family was just that way. Lila had her creepies; Mom, her wu-wu; Theo lived for music; and Isis was a net-surfing goth chick. And Daddy. Daddy had had his photography. Dee finished her turn and asked me again.

"Excuse me," Jared snarled. "Is anybody gonna ask me anything?"

"Sure thing, Daddy-o," Connor said. "Name your poison."

"Dare."

"Dare it is. I dare you to swim across the pond, fully clothed, shoes and all." Connor leaned back on his car hood and waited with a satisfied grin. Dee giggled.

Jared threw another pebble, hard and far. "That's not a dare, man. That's a camp activity. A dare should have, oh, I don't know, some aspect of the *daring* in it. Like . . ."

The sound of a train whistle broke through the canopy of trees. It would be down the track and rumbling by us any minute. A look I couldn't read passed over Jared's face. "I'll give you a dare." He took off running up the embankment. Within seconds he had clambered onto the

tracks and was standing there, completely still, a long-limbed scarecrow daring anybody to mess with him.

"All right, you've proved your he-man status. Now come back," I yelled over the growing train noise.

Jared didn't move. The train was inching closer, making the ground tremble. Dee grabbed the sleeve of my dress. I could feel her rising fear. Mine too.

"Make him stop, Kar."

Question was, how did you make Jared stop? Once he set his mind on something, there was no deterring him.

Connor was on his feet, pacing nervously. "Dude, I'd hate to think I just paid for your last meal, man. Why don't you come down? We should be getting back, anyway."

"A sentry does not leave his post, Major." Jared was saluting the oncoming train. "That's what the old man says. And he should know."

The words chilled me. The whistle of the train was close now. I could see the long metal snake creeping through the trees, seconds away. The high beams from the engine car flooded Jared with eerie light.

"Jared, cut it out!" I screamed. "Get down here now!"

Connor started up the small hill toward Jared. The train started honking wildly. Dee was screaming.

Connor slipped on the hill, sliding back to the bottom. I couldn't watch. Couldn't scream. Couldn't move.

At the last second Jared dove off the tracks, tumbling head over heels down the embankment as the train screamed past on its way to parts unknown.

Jared stood up and dusted off the knees and elbows of his too short suit. Flashing a brilliant smile, he said, "Now *that,* my friends, was a dare."

It took at least twenty minutes of dull conversation to get my heart rate down to five hundred beats per minute. Dee was comfy now, babbling about her favorite *Friends* episode, while I shot hate darts at Jared. I made a mental note to tell Jared what a royal jerk he was the second I got home.

In the meantime I needed to save this night from complete ruin. My brain was spinning as to how to get Dee and Jared together and away from us when Connor threw me for the second loop of the evening.

"Jameson. Why don't you take Dee home? You can use my car. I'll get it from you tomorrow." Connor drove a vintage 1968 Mustang that belonged to his dad. Jared was practically drooling over the keys. The rest of us had dropped off our cars at our houses.

"If you're sure that's okay . . . ," Jared said happily, grabbing the keys and making the motor purr into action. "Come on, Malloy. Shake a tail feather."

"He is soooo cute!" Dee mouthed to me silently. She

did a secret happy-boy cheer, then climbed into the Mustang with Jared. "How will y'all get home?"

"Don't worry about it," I said quickly. How would we get home? Change a pumpkin into a carriage? Connor could do anything, it seemed.

When we were alone, I sat on my rock again, drawing in the dirt with a stick. Connor sat down next to me.

"I don't know how to tell you this, but I think Jared likes you."

I looked up quickly. Of course he liked me. We were best friends. "Get real."

"Calls 'em as I sees 'em."

Jared like me? No way. "First of all," I said, "no. Second, no again. And third, Jared would have to be insane not to be into Dee. She's much prettier than I am."

Connor turned the X-ray vision on me. "Why do you do that?"

"Do what?" I poked at a big clump of dirt with my stick.

"Put yourself down."

"I'm not putting myself down. I'm just . . ." Just what? I couldn't finish that sentence.

Connor leaned forward with his elbows on his knees. He kicked a little dirt at my stick. "Look, I'm a guy. I can tell when another guy likes a girl. And Jared definitely has it for you. I can't blame him."

He couldn't? Suddenly it didn't matter if Connor was delusional about Jared. Connor liked me. He said so. Why didn't I have my camera with me, recording this moment for posterity?

Uncomfortable with the attention, I changed the subject. How retarded is that? "You know, this used to be the site of a makeshift graveyard during the Civil War. Some people say it's haunted. Isn't that interesting?"

"Very." Was it my imagination, or was he getting within kissing distance again? "Where'd you hear that?"

"From my . . ." A lump rose unexpectedly in my throat. "Just a story I heard."

Connor tucked his finger under my chin and lifted it. His eyelashes were impossibly long. "You can say it, Kari. Your dad told you that story, didn't he?"

"Yes." It was a whisper. "He told me a lot of stuff. I wish . . . I wish . . ." I couldn't finish. Big, fat tears rolled down my face, and I let them.

Connor didn't say a word. He didn't say he was sorry or try to make me feel better with that BS about my dad being in a better place now. I was vaguely aware of his jacket across my shoulders and his arms around mine.

For a minute I forgot about trying to be perfectly in control, and I told him about my dad wanting to be a photographer, about how much I loved him and how I thought I heard his electric razor some mornings or smelled his aftershave in the street. I told him stuff I hadn't said to anyone for four years. Not to Dee. Not even to Jared. Connor let it soak into him like needed rain.

After my emotional binge and purge, we sat quietly by the tracks in the long grass. Another train whooshed by, making me feel sleepy with its clackety-clack sound. The whistle pierced the night and left a lonely feeling on the air. The sound seemed to linger and fade into singing. At least someone was singing, and not very well. I felt Connor's jaw moving against the top of my head.

"'Gotta swing, Daddy-o, swing. Jump and jive. Gotta swing, Daddy-o, swing . . .'" It was a Robin's Hoods' tune. I turned around and could swear he blushed in the dark. "Yeah, I know. I suck. But I thought you could use a little comic relief."

A huge rush of hope fluttered around my rib cage. I didn't think I could love him any more than I did at that moment. I was wrong. Connor took my hand and stood me up. To my surprise, he didn't put the swerve on me. He took off his shoes.

I swallowed hard and tried not to come off as nervous. I took off my shoes, too. I wasn't sure what was going to happen. Next Connor put his left hand on my back by my waist and took my other hand in his. Then we started to sway. Left, right, left again as he hummed. He twirled me gently under his arm and said, "That's it. Now go right."

We were dancing. It was as beautiful as any Hollywood movie. Connor let go for a second, and I stumbled a little on a small, sandy hill. Laughing, Connor grabbed my hand, twirled me out, then pulled me close, my face right up to his. We stood there for an eternity, barely moving.

My mind kept asking the question, *Is he going to kiss me?* A tickly feeling started in my feet. Hey, some girls feel romance in their stomachs. I'm a foot girl. The tickle got more and more intense, almost a burning sensation.

Wait a minute. It *was* a burning sensation. The sandy hill was swarming with fire ants, and so were our bare feet.

"Yow!" Connor shouted, jumping about ten paces back. He hopped from foot to foot, trying to brush off the ants. I ran to the swimming hole and stuck my feet in. Connor followed. We looked like a couple of colorful waterbirds knee-deep in muddy water. So not the way I was picturing the end to my evening.

"Kari," Connor said after a minute.

"Yeah?" I asked.

"Strange things happen when you're on the scene. Did you know that?"

What did he expect? If you're gonna date an Odd Dobbins, you'd better be ready to deal with the weirds.

chapter 10

Let me just go on record as saying that on a scale of one to ten, the pain from fire ant bites rates about a twelve.

Connor's feet were so swollen and red, he could barely walk. He certainly wouldn't be swinging for a while. I found a phone to call Mom at a closed gas station, and she had to cruise down in the Jesus mobile and cart us home.

The whole way over to Connor's house he held my hand, giving it a little squeeze every so often. I would have endured bites by poisonous snakes to get to experience that again.

As I sat in the backseat with him, my hand in his, my feet swollen to twice their normal size, my heart danced in my chest. Connor had almost kissed me. He'd definitely meant to kiss me. And for the first time I felt sure that Nan was out of the picture and I was in. I couldn't wait to step into my Sweet Sixteen arm in arm with Connor. With any luck, my feet would be back to normal by then.

Mom and I helped Connor hobble up to his door. His mom must've seen us through the window because she flew to the door, looking freaked. "Honey, what happened?"

"Long story, Mom. Have we got any calamine lotion handy?"

"Sure," she said. Not "I don't know" or "Let's use tincture of newt." Just "sure," like normal moms across the globe do. She had us sit in the living room while she went to get the icky pink stuff.

If I thought the outside of Connor's house was gorgeous, the inside was even better. The kind of house that has books neatly stacked on built-in shelves with room for the occasional vase or silver box. There was room to breathe. Connor's mom returned with the calamine lotion and cotton balls.

"Let me put down some paper before you do that." Made sense. My mom would have dribbled it all over the carpet and left it there. I noticed that Mom's hands were still painted with stars and moons, and I wanted to wish a pair of gloves on her.

Connor dabbed the chalky goo on his feet and explained the whole fire ant story. He dabbed some on my feet, too, in a gesture that will go down in history as the most romantic use of calamine lotion. ". . . and then Mrs. Dobbins, here . . ."

Connor's mom looked at me strangely, then at Mom. "Marcia?"

Mom smiled weakly. "Hi, Mary Beth. How are you?"

Mom and Mrs. Reese knew each other? This was becoming what Dee would call "so Roswell." Connor seemed surprised, too.

"I'm sorry. I forgot to introduce y'all."

"I noticed," Mrs. Reese said. "And this must be your daughter."

"Kari," I said, offering my hand, which I hoped she realized wasn't painted or otherwise adorned with weirdness.

Mrs. Reese was smiling now. I could see where Connor got the killer pearlies. "Well, Marcia, I haven't seen you since law school."

My mouth fell open. Okay, the revelation department was working overtime. My mom the gypsy moth had been in law school? I couldn't wrap my mind around it.

"When were you in law school?" I asked incredulously.

Mom was adjusting and readjusting her many-layered skirt, a sure sign that she was tense. "Oh, in a former life."

"I'll say," Mrs. Reese continued. "I think I've got a picture of us at a freshman picnic for the public defender's office. Hold on." She pulled a leather-bound volume off the bookshelf and opened it to a five by seven. Three neat rows of law students smiled for the camera. A sign read Class of '79. I did a quick scan and found my mom. She was sitting with her legs crossed at the ankles like a debutante. Her frizzy hair was pulled back into a neat ponytail. She was even wearing pearls.

Connor said what I was thinking. "Wow. That's you, Mrs. Dobbins?"

My mom nodded. At that moment I was ashamed of her. And I felt awful about it. But why couldn't she have stayed in law school with her pearls and her pressed jeans instead of turning into the crazy lady everyone felt sorry for? Including me.

"Here's to old times, huh?" Mrs. Reese put the photo album back where it belonged. On the shelf. Then she added, "I was sorry to hear about Henry. He was such a good man."

Connor cut in. "Mom, I'm inviting Kari to our barbecue next weekend."

"What a great idea. We'd love to have you, Kari. And Marcia. Why don't you come? You could bring your mother. Is she still working with insects?"

Mom stood up. "That's awfully nice of you, Mary Beth. But you know, I've got this business now, and I never have a spare minute. Let me give you my card."

Please, God, let her be out of business cards. Let Mrs. Reese think she has a flower shop or a fruit stand. Anything but—

"Marcia. Psychic, astrologer, and tarot adviser. No reading too small. No problem too big." Mrs. Reese put the card in her pocket. It would end up in the trash later, I felt certain.

We made our way to the front door. I kept my eyes on the floor, hot with embarrassment.

Five blocks later my mom pulled the Jesus mobile into our familiar driveway and cut the engine. "Home again, home again, jiggety-jig. Oh, my, Theo forgot to put the trash out on the curb. . . ." Mom was doing her patented avoid-the-subject routine.

"Why didn't you tell me you were in law school?"

"It didn't seem important."

"Not important that you had a whole different life before?"

Mom rolled down her car window and settled in for a talk. She leaned back against the door and let the wind whip her kooky hair back and forth. "Honey, I was a law student for exactly two years. That's it. No big deal." Ever notice that when people say, "No big deal," it's usually a really big deal?

"Why'd you quit?"

"Did you ever order a cheeseburger, bite into it, and suddenly realize you wanted fried chicken after all?" She was doing the Mom confusing thing again.

"Mom. Don't get all wu-wu Chinese fortune cookie on me, okay?"

"What I'm trying to explain is that I discovered I didn't want to be a lawyer. End of story. If I'd gone on to practice law, I would have been miserable. Some of us aren't blessed by coming out of the womb knowing who we want to be, you know. We have to figure it out along the way." A leaf floated through my window and onto my shirt. Mom brushed it off without thinking. "You have to march to your own kazoo."

"I think the phrase is 'march to the sound of your own drummer.'"

She laughed. "As long as you're marching. Come on, let's go inside."

I was still feeling mad at her. "Honestly, I don't know how you and Daddy ever managed to stay together. Maybe if you'd been a lawyer, he wouldn't have had to work so hard. He could have been a great photographer." I wished I could have taken it back the minute it was out.

Mom was wearing her hurt face. "Oh, Kari, honey." She sighed. "Your dad . . ." She got quiet. A car passed by. She took my hands and stared at them, turning them over. Her hands glowed. The paint was neon. "Maybe you're right. But maybe, just maybe, Daddy worked so hard at the office because he wasn't brave enough to go after what he really wanted. Because maybe he'd find out he didn't really have what it takes."

I pulled back my hands. "That's not true. Daddy was supertalented."

Mom shrugged and fell back again. "He had a good eye for composition. He was certainly skilled. But to be a real artist, you need to capture people's souls. I remember one time—"

"I don't want to hear any more about this, okay?" I hobbled out of the car on my swollen feet.

Mom called after me, "Kari . . . please don't be mad." I knew she was sitting there, getting smaller and smaller behind me. But I felt like if I turned around, maybe I'd have to accept that she was telling me the truth.

But it wasn't true. I wouldn't let it be. Starting right now, the Odd Dobbinses were about to have a change of fortune. And it would start with my party. My glorious, normal party. And my family was going to play their parts. So help me God.

The next evening, once the dinner dishes were cleared away and piled in tipping towers by the sink, I sat everybody down at the kitchen table. An easel displayed the pie charts I'd spent most of the afternoon working on. There were two pie charts: one for party duty and one for dress code. I was leaving nothing to chance.

"Okay, let's recap. The party starts at eight. Food needs to be on the tables under the tent by seven-thirty, but not before."

"What if the dogs get to it?" Theo asked gleefully.

"Thank you. That brings me to an important party night rule. No animals of any kind. No creepy crawlies. No Hefty. No George. They've all got to have a reptile/mammal slumber party somewhere else."

"I will not ship out my family!" Lila hissed. She was eating pistachios and letting the hulls fall to the floor. Lovely.

"It's just for the night, Lila. And it's for their own safety. I don't want anyone kidnapping George 'cause he'd make a cool pet."

Lila looked horrified. "So we're agreed?" She nodded. "Mom, what time are Robin's Hoods coming on?"

Mom tapped her finger nervously against her upper lip. "Oh, I don't know. . . ."

"Mom. You did hire them, didn't you?"

"I'll do it first thing tomorrow. Last week Mercury was in retrograde and I couldn't get a thing done. Tomorrow. I promise."

"Don't get those swinging retards to play. Hire us," Theo suggested. He looked around the room for support.

"Yeah, right. Why don't I wear a sign that reads I'm a Big Dork," I snapped.

"I thought you already wore one of those."

Mom intervened. "All right. Truce. Go on, honey."

"Since this is going to be on film, I'd like to spruce the place up a bit. I've got a chart here that details who cleans what and what gets stored in the basement for the time being," I said, looking over at the stuffed deer head whose antlers were serving as a clothesline for Lila's freshly washed girdles.

Lila slammed her hand down on the table. "I will not have my home turned into a bourgeois training camp."

Mom cracked her knuckles nervously. "Mother . . . it's just for the night," she said in a little mouse voice.

"Hmmmfph!" Lila sniffed. "I want everything back in place the next morning."

I carried on. "Let's talk dress code. This is a dress-up party, and I've got some ideas for what to wear." I pointed to my pie chart that listed clothing combos. "Theo: button-down shirt, nice pants or khakis. Mom: that peach dress you wore to the Nelsons' wedding four years ago." It was a little out of date but tasteful. A holdover from when Daddy was alive. "Isis. Whatever you wore for your class picture."

Isis raised an eyebrow. "I burned it."

"Well, then you'll just have to wear something of mine. Lila . . ." Here came the hard part. Personally, I had never seen Lila in anything from this century. If I could just get her into something seminormal, it would do. "White shirt. Beige skirt. No wig."

Lila stood and threw her long, gecko-printed scarf over one shoulder. "I don't do beige. Good night, Mussolini. I'm going to bed."

On Monday morning the sun rose on career day at Greenway High. Counselors from schools statewide set up tables in the cafeteria to tell us about careers in exciting worlds like data entry.

Jared lived for career day. He went from table to table, signing up for info on everything from dental hygiene to selling insurance. While Dee was caught listening to a woman recruiting for flight attendants, Jared pulled me aside.

"Long time, no call. Plays with Matches feels settler woman angry."

It was true that I hadn't called him all day Sunday. I was still mad. "Nice stunt you pulled with the train."

Jared picked up a packet for design school. He leafed through it. "Mad about the train thing. Gee, I thought girls liked those wacky heroic gestures."

"Girls like heroic gestures, not moronic ones."

Jared looked kind of miserable.

Dee walked up. "I think I could make a career out of going to career day. Sheesh. What's that?" She pointed to the application for design school.

"Nothing," Jared said, then thought better of it. "Hey, Malloy, can you do me a favor? Can you keep this for me at your house? If my dad finds it in my room, he'll ship me off to he-man school."

Dee cradled the form as if it were a newborn. "Sure. Your dad searches your room?"

"The earring incident stimulated his military reflex. Now I get surprise searches to make sure I'm not hiding terrorists under the bed. Uh-oh, here comes trouble."

Jen Appleton and a gang of preppies were crossing the cafeteria. One of the kids had a boom box, which he plugged in.

"Hit it!" Jen cried. A Britney Spears song strained the boom box's tiny speakers. Jen and her friends had put their hair in pigtails like Ms. Spears herself. Now they were moving through some major dance steps and lip-synching. I realized they were doing the video. Thankfully, our principal, Mr. Jeter, pulled the plug on the act—literally.

"Jen Appleton, would you like a detention for disrupting career day?"

"You don't understand, Mr. Jeter. We're auditioning for Kari's movie." This explanation seemed to leave Mr. Jeter dumbfounded. He wasn't the only one. Jen turned to me. "What did you think? We'll be even better by your party."

How could I explain the concept of documentary to Jen? I had to try. "That was . . . really awesome," I told her. "But the thing is, um, this movie? It's a documentary. That means there's no script or dancing or auditioning. You just show up and be yourself."

Jen's fellow drill teamer cocked a hip out to one side. "Well, that doesn't sound very interesting. Just a bunch of teenagers talking?"

"Think about it," I said. "You can talk about anything you want to without having somebody tell you it's out-of-bounds."

I noticed Jared talking with Mark over by the vending machines. They seemed to be deep in conversation. Jared pointed in my direction. Oh no. Please don't tell me Jared was throwing me to Mark in retaliation for the Magnolia setup.

"But won't your parents be lurking?" the girl persisted.

Jen snorted unbecomingly. "There is nothing you could say that would be out-of-bounds in Kari's house. Her whole family is completely weird."

I could have held Jen's head underwater for a full ten

minutes. I pretended to ignore her. "My mom will be busy doing the mom thing—checking on the food and making sure the band has stuff to eat. She's the one who thought to hire Robin's Hoods, you know."

"Cool," said the cheerleader.

"Will your grandmother be stirring the cauldron?" Jen laughed, then turned a simpering smile on me. "Don't get mad. I'm just kidding."

Yeah, right. I forced a smile to match hers. "I think she'll be pretty busy talking to her casting director friend."

Jen's face froze.

"Listen, I'd better get going. Got some stuff I need to take care of," I said importantly.

And I did, too. Like finding a casting director, hooking up my best friends, and making sure my family didn't destroy me once and for all.

"Hey, Karnage, I found it." Jared beamed and held up a 1920s flapper dress for my inspection. "You can look like a mobster's girl."

Jared's car had broken down again. I offered him a ride home if he'd go with me to find my party dress. See, the very thing that most annoyed me about Jared—his uncompromising honesty—was also what made him a great dress critic. Dee or my mom would tell me everything

I tried on looked great. But if something made my butt look like a water buffalo, Jared would let me know.

I put the beaded number back on the rack. "Not the look I'm going for."

Rose, the proprietress, came out from behind her ancient cash register. She had to be somewhere between sixty and death. "What are you lookin' for, dahlin'?" she asked in a thick southern drawl.

Jared was surprised when I skipped the mall and drove us across town to a great vintage clothing store called Secondhand Rose. It was an amazing place. Like an old Hollywood wardrobe department. Racks of dresses and suits from every era lined the narrow shop.

Lila had been pretty psyched about this turn of events, too. So much so that she offered to pay for the dress. Shock of shockers. I guess she figured there was hope for me yet.

"Something from the forties." Then I added, "Something Betty Grable would have worn to a sock hop."

Rose gave a huge, nostalgic sigh. "They don't make 'em like her anymore. Come here, sugar. I know just the thing." Rose stepped over a couple of racks and started pulling things. "You about an eight?"

I nodded.

"Try these, honey. You can change right in there, then come out and model for us."

I shimmied into the first dress. It was dark green crepe. Jared hated it, said it was "too cafeteria lady."

The second dress was black and filmy. Jared said it was "beyond scary."

The third was a floral print. Jared said it reminded him of his grandma's kitchen curtains. I was starting to wonder why I'd asked him along.

The fourth dress had red cherries on a white background, a sweetheart neckline, pearl buttons, and a full skirt. He'd probably hate it, too, I figured, stepping into some red patent leather pumps. I swung open the dressing-room door.

"Well, what's wrong with this one?" I huffed, blowing a lock of hair out of my face. Jared just stood there, looking at me in a non-Jared way. It was a boy way. As in you-look-like-a-hottie boy way. I blushed. I felt like preening and running to hide in the nearest bathroom all at once.

"Dahlin', that is the dress!" Rose clapped in appreciation. Jared didn't say a word, just nodded slowly, then stuck his hands in his pockets and walked over to look at some Nehru jackets. It was Jared's seal of approval. The little bell over the door tinkled, heralding a new arrival.

"Well, hey there, dahlin'. How are you?" Rose said.

I peeked out from the dressing room to see Nan Tatum returning a primo men's 1940s dinner jacket,

total zoot-suit style. I ducked my head back in before she saw me but couldn't help watching with fascination through an opening in the curtain. Rose took the return. "You don't want this?"

"Let's just say I don't have anyone to give it to now." Even with no makeup, Nan was still beautiful.

Rose gave her a piece of paper. "There you go. Store credit. Have a nice day." The tinkle of the bell signaled the all clear. I took my new party outfit to the counter and handed it over to Rose, who wrapped the dress in layers of tissue paper.

I took a breath. "Excuse me," I said, pointing to the jacket Nan had returned. "How much is that jacket?"

"Sixty-five dollars. It's nice, isn't it?"

Sixty-five dollars? She might as well have said six million. Still, I could just imagine Connor's face as he opened the package and found it inside. Cut to hugely happy boy. Zoom in on major clinch. Hold on boy professing undying love to girl—who looks fabu in her new cherry print dress.

"Um, you know, I think I'll skip the shoes and take the jacket instead."

Rose smiled and wrapped up everything in a polka-dotted shopping bag. It was sort of icky of me, I know, but I couldn't wait to give Connor his present.

Jared was extra surly on the ride home. I tried to turn things around. "So. Talk to Dee today?"

"Yeah. I talk to her every day."

"She looked great today."

"She's pretty fine. No doubt about it." Jared poked his head into my glove compartment, looking for gum. He pulled out Lila's necklace and whistled. "Wow. Are you going to embalm me, too, if I, like, play the wrong radio station or something?"

"I might," I said, swiping the necklace and throwing it into my purse.

Jared found a stale stick of Juicy Fruit and popped it into his mouth, throwing the wrapper on the floor, which is what he did when he wanted to start a fight. Finally he said, "Don't you think sixty-five bucks is a bit steep for a guy you hardly know?"

I was tired of treading lightly around Jared. "I know I like him. Why do you have to be such a major pain about everything, Jared?"

"Because I hate to see you throwing this party like you're trying to win a prize."

"What do you mean?"

"It's like you've drifted off into John Hughes land or something. First of all, a documentary is supposed to be an honest, no-holds-barred exploration of an issue."

"Right. And I'm exploring Sweet Sixteen parties—"

Jared interrupted. "No. You're *packaging* your Sweet Sixteen party. You're using it to try to make yourself seem like somebody else."

I was really getting steamed. Being honest wasn't the same as being brutal. "Oh. I'm sorry. Did I break away from the Underachievers Club and leave you in charge?"

Jared snorted. "At least I know who I am. Here you are, carving your whacked-out family into a bunch of celluloid heroes so you can manufacture a happy ending. Get a grip, Kar. That's not art. That's a control freak's daydream."

All the blood in my body pooled in my feet. I stopped breathing. It wasn't a happy ending I was looking for. It was a happy beginning. Why couldn't Jared see that? I was so furious and hurt, I wanted to leave a mark on Jared's soul. "At least my dad wasn't embarrassed by me."

A muscle twitched in Jared's jaw, and I knew I had wounded him. It didn't feel like a victory, though. It felt awful.

I pulled into Jared's driveway, and he jumped out without saying a word. I watched him make the short walk up his front lawn in the shadow of a house that seemed to dwarf him.

chapter 11

I avoided Jared the rest of the week. I avoided thinking about him and the things he'd said. I didn't call him, and he didn't call me. Frankly, I was a lot happier that way. I could focus my energy on the Reeses' barbecue Saturday night and the much bigger party the Saturday after.

The Reeses introduced me to their friends as "Connor's friend Kari." It wasn't *girlfriend,* but it would do. Connor's dad was playing Lord of the Grill. It made me miss my dad. I helped Mr. Reese with the food while Connor went inside to help his mom.

Mr. Reese was flipping burgers like a pro.

"So I hear you're the granddaughter of the famous Lila Huntington."

Even when I thought I'd left my family at home, they followed me like a long, late-day shadow.

"She's a real kick in the head. I remember after the flood in '73, she put on some hip waders and went looking for a couple of her snakes that had gone missing. Scared the heck out of the whole neighborhood. How's she doin' these days?"

"Fine," I said, putting a bright copper spin on it. "You have a lovely home, Mr. Reese."

He put a few hot dogs down on the grill. They sizzled and popped from the heat. "Thank you. It's mostly Mary Beth's work. She's the decorator. You know, I always admired old Lila. And your mom. You know where you stand with those two. They do whatever suits them and don't worry about what the neighbors think."

No, they certainly didn't. That was my job.

"I understand your little brother and sister are real . . . individuals, too."

I swallowed the clump of hamburger in my mouth. "You could say that."

"How did you end up in that family?" He smiled and patted me on the back.

Connor strolled across the yard with two glasses of iced tea. He handed me mine.

"Can I borrow Kari for a bit, Dad?"

Connor's dad waved us on. Connor showed me around the house, then pulled me into a small home office. Silver-framed diplomas hung on every wall. A family portrait loomed over a fireplace. Connor, his mom and dad, and all the grandparents smiled down at me like those pictures that come with a new frame. "I hope my dad didn't bore you too much," he said, taking a sip of iced tea.

Boring? "He's great," I said. Connor's whole life was great. I decided this was the moment to give Connor the jacket. I wanted to see his face when he pulled it out and tried it on. "I have something for you."

Connor gave me a questioning glance. I practically ran to the bedroom where my purse was and grabbed the package I'd spent an hour wrapping. Back in the office, I watched him open it. His face was curious. Then shocked. Then glowing. I felt like I should say something. "It's to replace the one that died."

"This is the most amazing jacket I've ever seen. And you're the most amazing girl." Very tenderly, he kissed me. A long, satisfying kiss. I nestled against his chest. His heart kept time metronome style. Mine was beating wildly.

After an intoxicating minute Connor broke away. He slipped on his new jacket and smiled that smile at me. It looked stunning on him. The jacket, I mean. He wore it through the whole evening, even though it was pretty warm.

"I'm never taking it off," he said, weaving his fingers into mine as he walked me home after dinner.

"Might want to invest in some Lysol, then." I kissed him on his cheek and said good night. I couldn't remember feeling this happy, this normal before. It was like freshly laundered blankets, hot cocoa, and a Ferris wheel ride all in one.

Connor Reese. Kari Reese. Kari Dobbins Reese. Great filmmaking name.

But somewhere in the back of my mind, behind all the Ferris wheels and cotton candy, was the voice of Jared, the voice I'd been working so hard to avoid the last few days. The voice wanted to know where I got off giving Connor the jacket his *real* girlfriend had picked out for him.

When I walked through the door, my house was strangely quiet. Then I heard pounding from the backyard and headed outside. That's when I saw the tent. The elegant white canopy for my party had become a real, live circus tent. The multicolored kind with little fringe balls hanging off the top. I blinked hard and drew closer to the kitchen window. It was still there. An advertisement for Bolander's Plumbing ran around one side of it. Bolander's Plumbing—We'll Clear Your Pipes and Leave You Flush!

One thing. I'd asked Lila to do one thing—get the white tent from Ever's Hardware. My family was useless.

The sound of hammering filled the backyard. Rushing outside, I could see all four of the Munsters building what seemed to be an outhouse.

"How was the barbecue, honey?" Mom called out to me.

Lila cut in. "Never mind that. Grab a hammer, Kari Elizabeth. We need an extra hand for the bat house."

That stopped me. "Why do we need a bat house?"

Lila clucked her tongue at me. "For the shipment of bats, silly. They're arriving tomorrow all the way from Austin, Texas. Watch my thumb, Theodore."

I couldn't even digest that information. I was too fixated on the tent. I pointed to it. "What is that? Where's my white tent?"

Lila put some nails in her mouth and talked through clenched teeth. "White is so boring. This has character."

Mom jumped in to play peacemaker. Typical. "We thought it might look more interesting in your movie."

"*Interesting?* Mom, it has plumbing ads on it!"

"That's why we could get it so cheap," Lila explained.

"Hey, bummer about Levenger's," Theo said, pulling out a bent nail.

My mind was reeling. "What about Levenger's?"

Isis was stamping little bat images on a piece of old two-by-four. "They had a meltdown. All their freezers went out. They've canceled all orders for the next week."

This couldn't be happening. "So . . . what are you telling me?"

"No food!" Theo shouted.

"Darkness. Finality. Bleakness," Isis intoned with every stamp of her rubber bat.

I was screaming inside. I knew it wasn't my family's

fault that Levenger's wouldn't be able to cater my party, but I couldn't believe they weren't as panicked as I was. They just hammered away like it was any other day of the week instead of a full-blown crisis moment.

"Time-out!" I screamed. The hammering stopped. "I cannot have my friends over with this tent in the backyard. Please, please, please go down to Ever's and pick up the white one. I'm begging you."

Lila put her hands on her hips. She was exasperated. "This is a perfectly good tent, Kari Elizabeth."

Mom interrupted. "Maybe if we hang some lights on it . . ."

I was so frustrated that tears welled up in my eyes. They didn't understand. My voice was hoarse with tears. "Just once, I'd like for everything to be nice. Like when Daddy was . . ." I looked up at the starry sky and blinked to keep the sobs back. "He would have gotten me the white tent. Just because I wanted it."

Isis caught my eye. She was ready to cry, too. Mom kept kicking at the grass.

"It's just a stupid tent, Kari. Don't have a cow," Theo said. I could tell he was mad I'd brought up Daddy.

"Fine," I said, storming toward the back door. "I'll take care of it myself. Along with the food. And everything else in the world." I let the screen door slam hard

on its hinges and tried to remember that this was the day Connor Reese had kissed me.

Breakfast was unusually subdued at the Dobbins household. Lila took off the minute I walked in. That was fine with me. Mom sat at the kitchen table, reading a New Age rag and nursing a cup of tea. She handed me the number for Tokyo Joe's. Not this again.

"What's this?" I asked robotically.

"Lila talked to Joe last night. He said if you tell him what you want, he'll make it. Barbecue chicken. Ribs. Corn."

"A cake shaped like a big fish?" I couldn't help the dig. I was still raw about the tent.

Mom held her cup with both hands and stared into its depths like she was asking it the meaning of life. "A cake shaped like a cake." She nodded toward the menu that had a phone number scrawled on it. "That's his home number."

I felt a big surge of relief after I talked to Joe, who was totally nice about the whole thing and reasonable, too. Maybe I'd wear Lila's necklace around the house for a while today as a token of goodwill.

I was about to sit down to breakfast myself when the doorbell rang.

"I'll get it," I screamed, secretly hoping it was Connor. Then I remembered the bed-head crisis. "On second thought, Isis, can you get that?"

Without a word, Isis plodded to the door, cereal bowl and all. A minute later she said it was for me. Panicked, I grabbed Mom's old baseball cap off the counter to cover the terror that was my hair. When I got to the door, a man was standing there in a sports jacket.

"Hi. I'm Walter Garland from the *Greenway Gazette*. Are you Kari Dobbins?"

"Yes," I said hesitantly.

"Kari, my daughter Vanessa is in your class. She told me about this documentary you're doing. We thought it might make a nice story for our Lifestyles section. Would you be interested in having the *Gazette* come to the party to profile you and snap a few pictures?"

He could have been asking if I wanted to be on the cover of *Seventeen*. Maybe he wasn't a casting director for the WB, but a splashy story was just the sort of coverage I needed to make my application rock. A few lines of newsprint and voilà! Instant somebody.

Mr. Garland made plans to come a little before the party to set up. I couldn't wait to share the news. Back in the kitchen, I was greeted by an empty table and dirty dishes. I thought about calling Connor, but he'd

said they were going to Spartanburg to visit his grandparents for the day. The news was burning a hole in my throat. I had to tell somebody.

I ran upstairs and set up my camera. When the red light flashed, I grinned into the lens. "Okay. So here's an interesting turn of events. The local paper is going to cover me covering my class. Pretty cool, huh? Whoo-hoo!" That last part seemed so Campfire Girl. I'd erase it later and rerecord till it was perfect. Technically a documentary is supposed to be unrehearsed and totally real. Like a video diary. But I supposed it wouldn't hurt to erase one small part. Especially if it made the filmmaker look like an excitable dork.

I still had the urge to tell someone about the paper.

Carrying a peace pipe (otherwise known as Oreo cookies), I drove over to Jared's house. He was out front, mowing the lawn. For a second I didn't recognize him. He had his shirt off. His chest had filled out. A lot. For a second I understood why Dee had the hots for him. Embarrassed, I honked the horn. "Hey, Jameson! Get dressed. You're scaring the old ladies around here."

Jared cut the motor and pulled a Spiderman T-shirt over his head.

"Foot in Mouth brings peace offering to Plays with Matches," I said.

Over the proverbial cookies and milk, we made up. I told him all about the reporter, and he was jazzed for me. Jared hinted that he had big news, too. One of his comic books was going to be published, but that's all he would tell me. I tried to tickle it out of him, but he wouldn't budge. Mr. Jameson walked in mid-tickle fest.

"'Scuse me. Didn't mean to interrupt anything." He pretended to cover his eyes.

Jared jumped back. "I mowed the back. I've just got to finish the front."

"Don't worry about it, son. Paying attention to your girlfriend is more important, isn't it, Kari?" He winked at me.

"Kari's not my girlfriend," Jared growled.

"We're just good friends, Mr. Jameson," I said, trying to help Jared out by emphasizing the "friend" part. Parents could be so obnoxious at times.

An idea struck me, and I seized my chance. "Actually, one of the school's prettiest girls is, like, absolutely gaga over Jared." Jared shot me a warning glance. I ignored it. It was my girl prerogative. Plus mentioning it in public was a good way to goad him into asking Dee out, which he was clearly too shy to do on his own. "She told me she hopes Jared will bring her to my party."

Mr. Jameson was eating up the whole me-Tarzan, you-Jane thing. "Really? So, son. What are you waiting for?"

"I better finish the lawn before it gets too hot." Jared put his milk glass in the sink.

"Listen, Jared. You take my advice. Call that girl and ask her out. She's not gonna wait forever, you know."

Jared snorted. "You've never met Dee." He was in Obstinate Boy mode.

"I happen to know that your friend Mark is thinking of asking her out." I was winging it, trying to create a little jealousy action.

"You see there?" his dad practically shouted. "Someone else is already in line, waiting to advance. Are you gonna stay in the foxhole, soldier? Or are you ready to move out?"

"Does everything have to be a military metaphor with you, Dad?"

Mr. Jameson filled the door frame. His lips went tight and flat as fishing line. After a minute he said, "Do what you want. I'm through giving advice." He opened the fridge and pulled out some lemonade.

Jared let out a mournful howl. "Fine," he said, grabbing the phone. "I'll do it if it will make you guys happy. This could be the end of a beautiful friendship."

"You don't know that," I said coyly.

Jared fixed me with a look I'd never seen before.

"Don't you know it never works out when friends date? You've been watching the wrong movies, Kar."

I was fueling up for a battle when he laughed it off. He gave his best sexy eyebrow wiggle. "So. The newly scrumptious Miss Malloy wants me to put the swerve on her, eh? Live in fear, Greenway, live in fear."

Mr. Jameson slapped Jared on the back. "There you go, son."

I could literally hear Dee's squeal of delight when Jared asked her to my party. It wasn't a very romantic proposal. Just your basic nervous monotone delivered over the phone and all. It was Jared's style. But hey—he'd asked her out! I was psyched.

After he hung up the phone, Jared brushed past me on his way back to the yard and his lawn-mowing duties. I followed him out.

"Hey, Jared—"

Jared answered by starting up the lawn mower to drown me out. "Sorry, Karnage. Gotta get a mow on." He cut a clean line, heading toward the side of the house, and he didn't look back.

chapter 12

Before I could say "major panic attack," Saturday night had arrived with a beautiful white tent courtesy of Ever's Hardware and a sound system Theo had found through mysterious channels. I didn't care how he'd found it; I was just grateful. My little bro had even put on a tie for the event.

At seven-fifteen I took a deep breath and went to do a final check. I couldn't believe how great everything looked. With a massive cleanup and some votive candles, our house could pass for livable. I'd tacked up big swaths of white paper to cover the yellow walls and left markers for everyone to write down their random thoughts. The food table had a whole *House Beautiful* vibe. Lila's fat-bellied gods were doing duty as table supports. And Joe had come through with what looked like a yummy, nonfishy array of eats. Good, stick-to-the-ribs comfort food. It wasn't as fancy as Levenger's, but it wasn't bizarro world, either.

I hoisted up my camera and took a quick pan of the triple-layer cake decorated with icing roses, the platters of hors d'oeuvres, and the dozens of sodas on ice. Mom had bartered some tarot card readings with Joe for the extra layers on the cake. I wanted to capture this whole evening and play it again and again. My first real movie.

Isis brushed past me, carrying a tray of chocolate cookies she'd made herself. It was a little shocking to see her face. She'd pulled her hair into two ponytails that were just this side of Hello Kitty. But at least she wasn't wearing her standard ghoul makeup and black dress. Seeing her in my old denim jumper, which I knew she hated, made me feel kind of guilty about the way I'd treated her. I promised myself I'd spend more time with her when school was out.

"Thanks, Rach," I said, putting the finishing touches on a watermelon fruit bowl. "I mean, Isis. You're the best. Really."

She shot me a worried glance. Unexpected sentiment unnerved my baby sister. I gave her a hug, anyway, and went upstairs to inspect the troops. Lila had managed to find a tan—not beige—skirt, a white top, and a wig with a bun. It was like having Mrs. Butterworth spring to life, but at least it was seminormal looking. Mom had on her Sunday best. Well, what would have been her Sunday best if she went to church on Sundays. I gave her a kiss and thanked her for everything.

I felt pretty pleased with myself for pulling off the impossible makeover of the year, both the house and my family. Collecting bet money from Jared was going to feel pretty sweet, too. Soon we'd have a house full of teenagers talking about their lives. And I'd be able to look through my lens and focus on them completely without worrying that my life would crash down around all of us.

Mr. Garland arrived at seven-thirty with the *Gazette* photographer. They asked me to pose by the plywood bandstand that Jared, Dee, and I had built on Thursday night. It felt a little strange having the camera turned on me for once. I hoped my new dress would stand out in the black-and-white photos. I'd paired it with some black Mary Janes from the back of my closet and little white anklet socks, just like the swing dancers at Café Vortex. With any luck, the world would be introduced to Kari Dobbins, no longer an Odd Dobbins but a swank, together filmmaker on the rise. Please, please, please, I prayed.

Jared and Dee came right at eight. I showed them the house and the backyard. We sat by the food table and waited, listening to taped music over the sound system.

Dee kept picking at her cuticles. She only did that when she was beyond uptight. Jared played hovercraft by the chips and dip. They kept catching each other's eyes and looking away. It was beyond awkward, like they'd suddenly forgotten how to talk to each other. Hormones do strange things to people.

"Back in a minute," I lied, making a beeline for the house. The truth was, I was totally preoccupied with the party. In the kitchen I passed a guy I'd never seen before. He had thick, dark hair and a serious but nice-looking face. He seemed to be rearranging some crudités on a platter.

"Hi," I said, giving a slightly perplexed look at my very first, non-best-friend guest.

He looked up, then went back to fixing the platter. "Hi."

"Uh, can I help you?"

He shrugged and looked a little sheepish. "Just looked a little messy. I'm John." He extended his hand and gave me a firm, warm handshake.

"John. I'm Kari."

"Yeah, I know."

Okay. Not just every guy comes to a party to tidy up the plates. Very curious. "Do you go to Greenway?"

"Just started. Been living in Oregon with my mom."

"Oh," I said. The phone rang. "Excuse me."

It was Connor on the horn. "Listen, I'm running a little late, but I'll be there as soon as I can, okay?"

"No problemo," I said, although I was dying for him to get there.

I'd run out of things to fuss with, so I stood out on

our front porch and waited. Minutes ticked off my watch like gun blasts, and still nobody else had shown up. I trained my camera on the street, picking up the sounds of dance music from the backyard, and willed someone to arrive. A pair of headlights came around the corner, and my heart fluttered with excitement. I panned the street, dropping into professional mode.

"Well, it's eight-fifteen, and Skylark Drive is pretty quiet. Arriving late is apparently one of many Sweet Sixteen customs." The headlights headed slowly down my street. I couldn't quite see the car yet. Was it Jen Appleton? Connor? No, Connor would probably walk.

I was a little miffed that he hadn't shown up yet, that he was running late on the biggest night of my life so far. I swatted the feeling away like a gnat.

The headlights drew closer. "And here comes someone . . ." The car drove past us and down the street without stopping. ". . . else." A new panic gripped me to replace the old my-family-will-be-too-weird panic. What if no one came? I'd be massively humiliated. Beyond humiliated—I'd have to move to Mexico. Years from now the *Gazette* would run a whatever-happened-to article on Kari Dobbins, hostess of the only Sweet Sixteen party without guests.

Just then Mr. Garland stepped onto the porch from the side yard, startling me.

"Didn't mean to scare you. Say, what time did you say this party was starting?"

"Uh, between eight and eight-thirty," I said, stalling. I didn't want him to give up and leave.

He pulled my invitation out of his pocket. "Says eight."

"You know how it is with these wacky kids today," I said, forcing a brightness into my voice. "They all like to be fashionably late."

Mr. Garland checked his watch. "Well . . ."

I was just sinking into blankie-and-thumb mode when I heard car doors slam, followed by loud talking. A crowd of about ten of the drama kids, including Dave Kimball, wandered into the front yard. I started to breathe again.

"Excuse me," I said to Mr. Garland, who took a seat on the porch and fanned himself with his notebook. I practically leaped off the porch steps, then got ahold of myself. Coming off as a love-starved Doberman pup was not the image I wanted to convey.

"Hey, glad you could make it," I said coolly.

"Hey, Kari," Dave said. "Good tunes. Where's the party happening?"

"Actually, you're the first ones here," I said haltingly.

"Lame-o," mouthed a small girl with bright red

lipstick. I had to keep them from doing the old we'll-be-back-later thing.

"I'm glad y'all are here first. It gives me more time to get y'all on film without any distractions."

This made Dave preen like a peacock. He did a tight spin and struck a *Saturday Night Fever* pose. "Excellent," he said, dropping the pose. "Where's the food? I'm starving."

I pointed them toward the food table and waited for them to admire the careful menu selections. No one noticed. Instead they descended on the ribs and biscuits like vultures in party clothes.

Oh, well. I let them mill and talk and eat for a while, soaking up the night air and the dance music. When I thought no one was looking, I turned on the camera and started to film. Suddenly the party ground to a halt. They were staring right into the lens. Not exactly the natural teen state I was going for.

"Um, you know what? Can y'all just pretend I'm not here? Just go on and do what you'd do at any party, okay?" I gave them a second, then framed Dave and a girl named Alison in a tight shot. The cake was centered perfectly between them, giving the shot a nice balance. Pretty decent composition for a first try. Then I started listening to what they were saying.

Dave's voice trembled. "They don't know how long

she has. It could be a matter of weeks." He covered his face like celebrities do when they want the public to think they don't want their pictures taken, but you can still see them. A strangled sound came from his throat. Oh my God. Dave Kimball was choking at my Sweet Sixteen! Then I realized he wasn't in need of a Heimlich. He was crying. Fake crying. And not very well, either. I shut off the camera.

"Dave? What are you doing?"

He snapped to attention, all smiles. "Did you like it? I can cry at the drop of a hat. My drama coach says I'm a shoo-in for a soap."

Clearly Dave wasn't getting the whole real-life aspect of the documentary. He was treating it like one big audition tape. Fortunately more kids were drifting in. I grabbed a few—jocks, brains, and ravers for starters—and took them into the living room to shoot. Pulling out a stack of index cards with questions on them, I started firing away at my subjects.

"So, Ian, why do you think Sweet Sixteen parties are important?" I asked a raver in baggy cords and flannel.

"I don't know." He shrugged. "Something to do. Not a whole lot of that in this town."

"Dude." His lanky friend laughed. "That was such a stupid answer."

"No such thing as a stupid answer," I said. "It's a documentary. You say what you feel."

"Cool," Ian said, nodding thoughtfully. "Then I stand by my original statement."

"It's a total rite-of-passage thing," a girl named Sarah broke in. She was currently in the running for "most likely to become class valedictorian." "I mean, one minute you're a kid, and the next you have a driver's license. You hold other people's lives in your hands from that moment on."

"Or it could just be a great excuse to shop and make your parents crazy." Swinging the camera around at the sound of his voice, I caught Connor leaning against the bookcase. I literally stopped breathing. He was wearing the jacket I'd bought him. A corsage box was in his left hand. The reason for being late, no doubt.

Instant forgiveness, coming right up. He walked over and pinned a beautiful spray of sweetheart roses on my collar. The raver dudes snickered, and my face went hot and numb.

"Keep going," Connor whispered. "You're doing great."

I turned the camera on him. I asked the next question playfully, but I really wanted an answer. I don't know why it felt so important to me. But it did. "So tell me, where do you see yourself ten years from now?"

"Bogus question." The answer didn't come from Connor but from a guy in the corner. John. The anal-retentive, food-arranging guest I'd met earlier. It stung to have my carefully thought out question called bogus, especially in front of the crush of my life, but I had to keep my cool. I was a professional now.

"John, right?" I asked icily.

"Right."

"Okay, John. You're on."

"It's just that everybody assumes life starts when you get out of high school. Like what you're doing now is pointless or something. It's so condescending."

Sarah broke in. "Exactly. Everything is geared toward preparing you for some future you can't even, like, get a handle on, it's so nebulous."

A jock in the corner spoke up. "And then your parents tell you to enjoy high school because it's the best time of your life."

More kids were crowding into the living room and voicing their thoughts. It was just what I was looking for—a window into the minds of sixteen-year-olds.

"So . . . ," I started, hoping a question would come to mind to keep the energy flowing. "Is that what Sweet Sixteens are all about? Finding the best time of your life? Doing something that isn't pointless?"

"It's about making out!" a bandie in a yellow button-down shouted. There was a chorus of laughter. I didn't want to lose everybody, though.

"Seriously," I said.

"Seriously." It was John again. "Do you have to have a reason to party?"

Irritation crept into my voice. "Well, yeah. Don't you?"

"No, man. I think that's the point. That for one night you can just be sixteen. Do a cheesy line dance. Ask a girl out." He fixed me with what felt like an X-ray stare. "You don't have to prove anything."

Who was this guy? Why was he challenging me in *my* movie at *my* party?

For some weird reason, his comment left me feeling unbalanced, like a door with a loose hinge. I wanted there to be a rhyme, a reason, and a reward for everything. For misfit daughters. For dads who died young. For loneliness. A party wasn't just a celebration—it needed to mean something, to get you somewhere.

Jen Appleton intruded on my moment. As usual, she was three steps behind the conversation. "You know what I want to be when I grow up? An anchorwoman. Just like Kathie Lee Gifford. I could have my own talk show." She was really mugging for the camera. I didn't have the heart to tell her that getting close to the lens

was *so* not flattering. Plus she had chocolate crumbs on her mouth. Every time I'd seen her, she'd been scarfing down another one of Isis's cookies.

"You know that 'talk show' means the guests talk and you listen, right?" John was grinning. He had a nice smile, I realized. Not as devastatingly wow as Connor's, but sweet and sincere.

Jen gave John a fiery glance. "Whatever." She sat down next to me and whispered in my ear, "Kari, I thought you said there would be a casting director here."

She caught me off guard. In the corner Mr. Garland was taking notes. He gave me a small wave, which gave me a desperate idea. "Don't look now," I whispered back. "But check out the guy in the corner." Well, it wasn't technically lying. Of course, Jen looked right away.

"Excuse me," she said, straightening her hair and making a beeline for Mr. Garland. I hoped she would be her typical self and talk a lot so she wouldn't find out who he really was.

Relieved, I caught Connor's eye and noticed Nan Tatum hovering in the hallway. She stalked off toward the backyard, but not before I registered how fantastic she looked. Sleek and sexy and ultracool. Not all geeky like me in my 1940s dress. I suddenly hated what I was wearing down to my pristine white socks. I was

America's dorkiest sweetheart. Nan was a screen goddess. I wondered if Connor had seen her, too.

Before I could agonize too much longer, Scott the zoot suiter rushed me. Cheryl and Charlotte, his silent backup singers, were right behind him. He practically threw a yellow flyer at me.

"I thought you were on the level."

"I am." *And while we're at it,* I added silently, *what's with the old movie dialogue? Annoying much?*

"Read the flyer."

Big, block letters announced a gig by Robin's Hoods at Café Vortex on Saturday, May 12. As in tonight. My mind reeled. How could they possibly play a gig at Café Vortex and my party on the same night unless . . . I ran through the house, looking for my mom, and finally found her in the kitchen, doing a tarot reading for Dee, who was noticeably without Jared. I showed Mom the flyer.

"Mom, please tell me this is a mistake. Please. I'm begging you." Mom drummed the table with her fingers. That was all the confirmation I needed. "Oh my God. I'm dead. I'm, like, put a tag on my toe and roll me to the morgue, so dead."

"Honey, calm down," Mom said in that let-me-kiss-your-boo-boo-and-make-it-better way. "They were

already booked. I'm so sorry. But I hired another band that I hear is even better!"

"Who?" I wailed. Loud feedback screeched through the sound system. A familiar voice boomed out.

"Hellooooo, Greenway! Are you ready to rock? Give it up for Ina Goddah Nagilah!"

The first screeching sounds of Ina Goddah Nagilah's own anthem, "Fish Sticks Make Good Eatin'," came blasting over the sound system. No wonder Theo had set it up. Mom had hired his band!

This couldn't be happening. My brain would not process such tragedy. Ever have one of those nightmares where you try to scream and nothing comes out? That's how I felt standing on the back porch, watching seven scrawny seventh graders playing a hard-rock polka to a totally stunned sophomore class. The face of every sixteen-year-old wore the same dazed, disaster-movie expression. Clarinet in hand, Theo took the mike and began to sing in his achy-breaky voice.

"Fish sticks make good eatin' / That's what the hair net ladies say / Wednesdays, you get mystery meat / Fridays, you get fish sticks on your tray. . . ."

Theo strutted and pranced like a cross between a rock star and a chicken. It wasn't pretty. He came in on his clarinet solo while the drummer was still doing his solo. In fact, everyone in the band seemed to be trying to grab his fifteen minutes of fame at the same time. The result wasn't so much a song but a train wreck with a beat.

A few of the bandies in the crowd started cheering and yelling, "Sing it, brother!" A lot of kids were laughing and pointing. Some started drifting out to their cars, disappointed that Robin's Hoods weren't there.

Dave Kimball sulked past me on his way out. "I thought this was a movie party."

"It is," I practically screamed. "Forget about the band. Come on. I'll interview you on camera."

"Ask me a bunch of boring, canned questions? Forget it. I'd rather watch *Baywatch*."

"They're not boring questions!" I yelled desperately. Scanning the crowd, I searched anxiously for some way to stop the leakage of party goers and caught sight of Nan, looking smug and self-satisfied over my plight. It was the second time I'd been disgraced in front of her.

Suddenly Jen Appleton doubled over and ran for the bathroom. "I'm gonna be sick!"

"It's not my fault!" Isis blurted out instantly, which meant that it was.

"What did you do, Rachel?" I demanded, grabbing her arm. "You've got to tell me."

"It was just a joke." She put the snarl back in her voice, but her eyes were scared.

I yanked her into the kitchen. "What did you do?"

She broke away. "Why do you have to be such a control freak all the time?" She was starting to cry.

"I'm not a control freak. . . ."

"You are too! You're all, *Rachel, wear your hair this way. Rachel, why can't you be like you used to be?* And then you embarrassed me in front of my friends and sent them home that night." She was morphing into the little girl she really still was.

"Are you going to tell me what you did? Or should I get Mom?"

She practically spat at me. "I baked a box of Ex-Lax into the cookies."

"You what?" I screamed.

"Well, how was I supposed to know it could make you really sick? I thought it would just, you know, make you go a lot."

"Oh my God." I put a hand over my eyes. "Come on," I said, grabbing her by the arm again. When we got to the bathroom, Jen was lying on the bathroom floor, moaning and holding her stomach.

"Man, it stinks in here," Isis commented. I shushed her.

"I think I'm dying," Jen wailed.

I handed her some Pepto-Bismol. "You're not dying. I promise."

"You and your freakazoid family tried to poison me. And that wasn't a casting director—he was Vanessa Garland's dad. He writes that cheesy Lifestyles column. You're so full of it, Kari Dobbins. Ohhhh!"

"Maybe if you hadn't eaten half a dozen cookies by yourself, you wouldn't be so sick. Did you ever think of that?" Isis chimed in.

"I only had one!"

Isis found her surly button again. For once I was glad. "You ate six while I was watching you. Do they kick you off drill team for that?"

"Don't you talk to me that way, you . . . you . . . vampire girl!" Jen's face went a little pale. She put a hand on her stomach. "Oh no. Not again." Isis and I took that as our exit cue. Isis burst into tears.

"I didn't mean to ruin your party, Kari. Honest. Please don't hate me." Tears rained down her face. Her wet cheeks still had some of their baby fat, I noticed. Without all that cakey makeup, she was small and round and clean as a Sears catalog doll.

I was so mad, I wanted to give her the silent treatment till we were fifty. But I had to admit that I'd been

pretty high-handed about her friends. The whole night was so wild and mixed up that yelling at Isis wasn't going to solve anything.

I put my arm around her, and she let it stay. "It's all right, Rach. It was a stupid prank. You have to tell Mom, though, so she can help out Jen, okay?" I sent her off to get Mom and wondered what I could do for damage control. What did directors do when a set went crazy? They shut down production. Not an option. I had to get Theo off the stage and get some real music on fast.

The famous disappearing Mr. Jared Jameson poked his head in the screen door. "Uh, Karnage? Are you having the same bad dream I am?"

"Yeah, and I can't wake up."

Jared took pity on me. "Don't worry. I think the worst is over."

Theo's voice cracked and warbled through his microphone. "Ladies and germs, would you please join me for the Sweet Sixteen pledge of allegiance?"

Sweet Sixteen pledge of allegiance? I didn't know what it was, but it didn't sound promising. A drumroll announced something big. I pushed through the screen door in time to see Theo and his band mates ripping off their shirts with rebel flair. KARI 16 was scrawled across their scrawny, hairless chests in Magic Marker,

immortalizing my name and my disaster in one pure moment. Theo had vowed revenge, and he was getting it. In living color.

One of the guys from the wrestling team started cat-calling. "Hey, girls, time to hit the weights!"

That's about the time I wished I'd lose consciousness. Ina Goddah Nagilah responded with a death wish. Theo pumped his arms and squatted like a sumo. "Hey, look! I'm on the wrestling team." He laughed.

Wrestler Boy wasn't amused. "You better watch yourself if you know what's good for you."

I knew I needed to do something. But I was paralyzed. Rooted to my patch of grass while my own brother set anarchy in motion.

"Oooooh, Mommy, I'm scared of the big, bad, wrestling girlie man," Theo whined. Then he launched into a full repertoire of gross grunting and pig noises. The whole band followed suit. Oinks and belches and high-pitched reet-reet-reets screeched over the PA.

"Quick!" I shouted to Jared. "Turn off the mike and put the house music back on." Good thought. About two seconds too late.

Wrestler Boy let loose with a holler that, actually, sounded a lot like Theo's imitation. "I'm gonna teach you some respect, boy." He ran screaming up onstage,

tackling Theo, who was just wiry enough to slip out of his meaty grasp.

"Missed me, girl wonder!" Theo was overjoyed with himself till the rest of the wrestling team got in on it. With a collective war cry four enormous wrestlers jumped the stage. A look of total fear lit the faces of Theo and his band mates. They took off fast, knocking over the microphone and the drum set along the way. Everyone stood watching, slack jawed.

"Come on," I said to Jared. "Help me turn on the music." We ran for the jumble of equipment at the back of the stage. A bloodcurdling scream erupted from somewhere in the yard. I looked up to see Theo's drummer jumping out of what he had thought was a toolshed. He'd tried to hide in Lila's bat house.

"Aaaaahhhhhhhhh!" He whooshed past like a bullet. I could hear a horrible screeching, and then they came.

Mental note on recipe for disaster: Start with one out-of-control party. Add dozens of black, winged creatures rumored to be bloodsuckers. Mix well.

The sky was thick with shrieking, flapping bats, swooping through the crowd. Kids started running pell-mell out of the backyard, bouncing off each other like some live-action pinball game.

"Get them off me! Get them off me!" A girl was freaking

near the amplifiers even though nothing was chasing her.

"You're okay. They're not carnivorous!" I shouted through the din. She responded by falling on the ground and rolling over and over as if she were putting out a fire.

I had to stop things from totally going nuts. I grabbed the mike. "It's okay, everybody. Really. They're more freaked out than you are, I promise." I didn't think that could possibly be true, but I had to act fast. Kids were climbing over each other to get inside.

I think that's when the dogs got out of the house. Our huge, lumbering mutts, who had the combined brain-power of an acorn squash, thought this was the best game they'd ever played. They chased everything that moved and barked up a storm. Of course, nobody else knew they were just sweet morons. Usually big dogs charging full speed ahead equals panic. Like we needed any more panic.

I grabbed for Fric and fell to the ground. "Get over here, you mangy mutt. Fric! Fric, come! Now!"

One of the swing girls, I think it was Charlotte, was headed straight for the lever that triggered Lila's underground sprinkler system.

Please. No. "Watch out!" I screamed, just as she tripped over it. The sprinkler came on full force. I had never seen so much water in my life. Everything was getting drenched, and with all those people running around, the ground was turning into a muddy mess. Fric and Frac ran toward me with their filthy paws.

"No! No! Down! Down!" I yelled, backing away from them, right into the food table. I watched helplessly as my beautiful three-layer cake toppled over and landed decoration side down. Frac lapped at the icing roses till there was muddy cake all over his nose.

Tears filled my eyes as I bent down and picked up a section of cake like I could save it. HDAY RI, it read. Theo zoomed past, wearing a huge grin. The little jerk was enjoying my misery. Wrestler Boy was hot on his tail. Theo slipped in the mud and took a spectacular slide into what was left of the tent. Still cradling the cake lump in my hand, I waved a mental bye-bye to my deposit as the tent collapsed onto mud and food and dogs. Wrestler Boy made a dive for Theo and ended up taking out a couple of football players like they were bowling pins. The football players didn't take kindly to being covered in mud.

That's how the food fight began. A raver grabbed the hunk of cake from my hand and bent his arm back catapult style. "Nooooo!" I shouted, making a dive for his arm. He lunged forward, throwing it, and I nearly fell face first into the mud. That was all it took. Hors d'oeuvres, corn on the cob, even chunks of watermelon zipped through the air, landing with splats and poofs on

taffeta dresses and brand-new khakis. A BBQ short rib smacked Dee in the face. After a stunned minute she grabbed a handful of slobbery cake and hurled it at Jen Appleton, who'd hobbled outside. Jen burst into angry sobs and threatened to kill Dee, which was kind of like threatening bodily harm to a Disney animal.

It was too much. My mind couldn't take it. It was floating numbly, about ten feet above my body and the total bedlam surrounding me.

"Stay away from my bats, you bourgeois hooligans!" Lila was running through the muck in her nightgown, wielding our kitchen broom like a machete. Somehow it wasn't the time to point out that *bourgeois* and *hooligans* were a contradiction in terms. Honestly, if I lived to be 112 years old, I'd never get over the sight of Lila storming the crowd in her purple polyester shortie. A few kids stopped throwing food to laugh and point.

I wanted to die.

A siren pierced the chaos. Make that sirens, plural. Someone had called the cops. Ten of Greenway's finest were taking in the scene and scratching their heads, trying to figure out whom to arrest first. They settled on Lila. I was torn between wanting to be a good granddaughter and come to Lila's aid and pretending I'd never seen her before in my life.

Good won out. "Excuse me," I said to a blond officer. "She didn't do anything. She's just a little wacky, that's all."

Lila started cursing a blue streak, which further humiliated me. The blond cop kept writing something on a clipboard. "You can make a statement if you like, miss. But she's disturbing the peace. We have to take her in."

There wasn't any peace to disturb. There never had been any at our house. "You don't understand. It's my fault. I wanted to have a party and . . ."

Another cop yelled, "Bob—give me a hand, will ya?" Bob went to join his friend, who was trying to restrain Lila. It took two of them to carry her to a waiting cruiser. The police were pulling kids apart and hauling the really rowdy ones off to a paddy wagon parked in the driveway. Theo marched past in custody. He was caked in mud and bits of food. I ran after him.

"Theo! Where do you think you're going?" Okay. It was a pretty stupid question, but my brain wasn't functioning at all anymore.

Theo was having the time of his life. "Whoo-hoo!" he shouted to no one in particular. "I'm gonna do some time!"

"Only till we find your mom, son," said one of the officers in a tired voice.

A policeman paraded Jen down the driveway. "But Officer," she wailed, "I'm, like, a total victim here."

"We'll sort it all out at the station when you've had a chance to calm down, miss," he answered. I didn't think I could handle another face-to-face with Jen Appleton that evening. I tried to sneak away and hide behind a parked car, but I wasn't fast enough. Jen pointed at me and screamed in hysteria.

"You! Kari Dobbins! You're a big, fat liar and a loser. You are so through at this school, it's not even funny!" I wasn't laughing. The cop pulled her gently along. Jen let out a final whimper. "These were my very favorite shoes!"

A flash went off and made me jump. When my eyes refocused, I saw the *Gazette* photographer snapping away. Oh my God. Mr. Garland was trying to get quotes from the police officers. I ran to stop him and fell over Fric and Frac right into a big, muddy grass puddle.

I looked down. The dress I had imagined dancing in all night long was now a vintage mess. "Mr. Garland," I called from my spot in the mud, "what are you doing?" Stupid questions were flying out of my mouth at an astonishing speed.

"I'm filing the best story to hit Greenway in ten years," he answered. He was nearly out of breath.

"Please, Mr. Garland," I begged, running after him and pulling bits of grass out of my wrecked hairdo. "You can't publish this story. Please don't."

"Sorry, Kari. I report the truth. You're a documentary filmmaker. You should know all about that. Excuse me, Officer . . ."

Okay. Technically he was right. But what was the good of making movies if you couldn't turn the lens on life and make it seem better than it was? If you couldn't make yourself into the girl everybody wanted to know instead of Odd Kari Dobbins, big-nosed geek?

I buried my face in my hands and wished that my dad were there to make everything right. He never would have made such a mess of things. I ached to have him put his arms around me and say, "Well, Boo, when you doooze it, you doooze it up right." A dull, thudding ache began to expand inside my rib cage. I needed something, one thing, to salvage the night. Someone to say, "Hey, it'll all be okay."

I scanned through the paddy wagon crowd for Connor, but I didn't see him. The throng in the backyard had dwindled down to a couple of animal control guys, Mom, and Isis. Mom called to me, but I had to find Connor. In the kitchen I appraised my mud-encrusted state. Not appealing. A quick rinse off and into some fresh, warm clothes, and then there might still be a chance to run off with Connor for a sane cup of coffee away from this insanity. Maybe I could even find the stomach to laugh a little at the whole mess.

It was Jared I ran smack into first. He had been baby-sitting my camera. "Some director you are. The best action scene since *Die Hard,* and you don't even have your camera. Don't worry. I got as much of it as I could. I like the female mud wrestler look, by the way."

I didn't have time for Jared's sarcasm. "Have you seen Connor?"

He gave me a pained look. "Kari . . ."

"What?" I asked irritably.

Jared put down the camera and headed for the front door. "Nothing." Great. Now my best friend hated me, too. Was there anything else that could possibly go wrong? I wanted Connor. The need to see him was like an aching in my joints. Shower. Jeans. Connor.

Rounding the corner, I saw Connor first. Then I saw Nan. They were coming down the stairs together, holding hands. For a second I stopped breathing, like the time Theo threw a football and hit me in the stomach by mistake. Seeing Connor hold Nan's hand like he'd held mine only a week ago snatched the breath right out of me.

I wanted to tell myself it wasn't true. That he was telling her good-bye forever in a noble manner. He was letting her down easy, saying things like, "It's over between us, Nan. Kari and I were meant to be. I see that now." But the churning, twisting heat deep inside

me told the real story. This wasn't good-bye. I was.

I couldn't let them see me like this, covered in mud and grass, my eyes stinging with tears. It was too pathetic. If there was one thing I couldn't deal with, it was pity from the guy I'd totally fallen for. I slipped quietly into the kitchen, stifled the desire to burst into tears, then put on my best wasn't-this-a-wacky-gas-of-a-party face. I "accidentally" bumped into them in the hallway by the framed print that hid Isis's corkboard.

"Oh, hi!" I said. The good cheer sounded hollow in my ears. "Y'all missed a wild time out there! I haven't laughed this hard in years!"

Connor and Nan seemed spooked but tried to act casual. "I wondered what all the sirens were about," Connor said. "That's why we . . . I came down."

"I better go find Jen," Nan said. She gave me a little smile on her way past. I couldn't tell whether it was a victory smile or whether she really felt sorry for me. And frankly, I didn't know which was worse.

Connor took off his fedora and ran his fingers over the brim. "You figured it out, didn't you?"

A lump grew in my throat. "You and Nan? Yeah. I mean, I always figured y'all would get back together sooner or later. No big deal." It was the biggest lie I'd told so far.

A sheepish smile tugged at the corners of Connor's perfect mouth. "You are so amazing. You know that?"

"Yeah, well . . ." My face hurt from holding back tears. I stared at the digital clock on the VCR, willing them not to come. It was nine thirty-three. The time of my dumping.

"I think you're *too* amazing for me, really." Oh God. Not the you're-too-good-for-me line. If he said we'd always be friends, I'd lose it. "It's just that, you know where you're going and who you want to be. You're so rational, so motivated. You don't need anybody. Nan is sort of whacked and all, but she needs me. I don't know. I can't explain it." I watched the hat moving back and forth in his hand. "I'm sorry. I hope you don't hate me for the rest of your life."

I wished I could hate him. That would be easier than feeling my heart hurt every time he gave me that better-luck-next-time smile in the halls or tried to be overly friendly so he wouldn't hurt my feelings.

I didn't need anybody? Had he really said that? I felt like one big black hole of need.

"Don't be stupid," I said. It came out a little harsher than I meant it to. Connor registered a startled expression. I laughed and poked my finger into his chest like a good sport. "I could never hate you." *Now, if you'll excuse me, I'll just run upstairs and sob into my pillow till I die.*

"You're the best," he said. "Thanks for the jacket." He kissed me on the cheek. The official you've-been-dumped seal.

I busied myself straightening the notepad and paper by the hall phone while I listened to Connor's footsteps walking toward a life with Nan and away from me.

By the time I hit my room, my whole body was heaving with sobs. I curled up on my bed, muddy dress and all, and hugged my pillow tight.

I'd made a royal mess of everything. My friendships. My party. My crush. My future. And tomorrow it would hit the paper for everyone to read about. One more feather in the Odd Dobbinses' cap.

I guessed I wasn't so different from my family after all.

chapter 13

Mom sat on the bed and rubbed my back like she used to do when I was little and my stomach hurt.

"Mom, can I go away to school next year?"

Mom stroked my head. "Where would you go?"

My voice sounded tired and flat. "I hear Siberia has some high schools. They don't know about my party. Yet."

I could feel her smiling at me. "It's cold in Siberia. You'll need a good coat."

We sat on the bed being quiet for a long time. In spite of everything, it felt good. Just Mom and me and the silence. Finally she stood up.

"I've got to go get Lila and Theo out of jail. I suppose I'll never hear the end of this. But watching Lila being carried away to a paddy wagon in her nightgown, well . . . It was worth it." She paused at the door. "You know, any girl who can throw a party that exciting ought to make movies or something." And she was gone.

I closed my eyes and sank into a restless sleep. I

don't remember much about my dreams, except that I was running and no one was chasing me.

The next morning Isis left the *Gazette* outside my door with a yellow sticky note that said, *Look! You're a star.* I didn't know which was more shocking, the fact that my Sweet Sixteen had made the front page with the headline Local Party Goes Batty or that Isis had used an exclamation mark.

I sank to the floor and read the whole article, reliving every agonizing moment. They'd even managed to compile quotes from various sophomores. Ninety percent of the kids voted it the worst party they'd ever attended. But a few kids called it "awesome," "rockin'," "hilarious," and "subversive." Words floated back to me. "It's just a party." Who had said that? I couldn't remember. It didn't matter.

Theo, Mom, and Lila were sitting in the living room when I came downstairs. Lila was giving Mom an earful about the indignities she'd suffered in jail. Meanwhile Theo was reveling in his new notorious status via the phone. ". . . and then I asked them to fingerprint me. Dude, I am on my way to becoming a rock-and-roll legend!"

Lila wasn't so thrilled. "I'm going to have to pay a fine to get my bats back, thanks to that bourgeois function of

yours, Kari Elizabeth. I told you this wasn't a good idea, didn't I?"

I didn't have the energy to fight Lila. Not this morning. Surprisingly, it was Mom who came to my defense, and I saw faint traces of the lawyer she once thought she wanted to be. "Mother, that's enough."

Lila's mouth screwed up like she'd swallowed a large dill pickle whole. "I did not raise you to speak this way to me."

"On the contrary, Mother. You raised me to be exactly this way." Mom turned her back on a slack-jawed Lila and grabbed a broom. "I'm going out to earn some good karma points by cleaning up the backyard, if anyone would care to join me." Mom sailed out the back door, trailed by Theo and Isis.

"I'm looking for souvenirs to add to the rocker mystique," Theo said, lumbering after Mom. "These babies should go for a fortune someday on eBay."

I probably should have helped out, but I was still nursing my wounds. Up in my bedroom, I stared at my video camera, working up the nerve to view the heinous party footage. Faces, places, and chaos swirled past on fast-forward, a blender effect of images.

Finally I came to a part I didn't remember shooting. It was Jared, sitting by himself in my room. I rewound and pressed play. The playback showed him leaning forward, elbows on knees, hands dangling, a few unruly bangs hanging over his eyes. "Hey, Karnage. I don't usually go for the high school confidential factor, but, uh, here goes. You asked a question tonight, about what we want to be when we grow up. The thing is, I mean, the really funny thing is that I want to be with you. That would have been my answer. If you'd asked me. And if I'd had the mojo to answer. Which I didn't. In fact, I'll probably erase this. If I can figure out how. Mechanical know-how not being my strong suit. Kind of ironic when your dad is Master of the Radio Shack Universe, huh? I guess I always wanted to tell you. . . ." The tape cut to static and snow.

I played it two and then three times. Jared. Liked. Me. When had this happened? I thought back to that day in Rose's store when he saw me in my party dress. The look on his face. The blush on mine. I felt like an idiot for not catching it and a double idiot for trying to pair him with Dee. My screwups seemed to be growing exponentially. Jared and me. Jared and Dee. Dee and me.

Jared likes you. That's what Connor had told me. And I had ignored it and gone after the guy who shared my zip code but not even remotely the same universe. Story of my life. Reach for the stars, miss, land squarely on butt.

Jared. Surly, smart, annoying, wonderful Jared. I let myself consider it. A close-up of Jared's face filled my head. The movie was rolling. He was decked out in his seersucker suit and tie. Music played as he leaned in, closer, closer, closer. I reached forward and my lips found . . . his cheek. It was like kissing my brother. No sparks.

With a cloud over my heart, I grabbed my keys and trudged off to either win back a friend or lose him forever.

Jared's mom said he was at Zippo Comix for some comic book signing. On the drive over, I couldn't stop thinking about Jared's confession. Honestly, a part of me enjoyed having him like me. I mean, Jared didn't like most people, so I figured I had to be a little special.

It was funny. I'd wanted people to see some magic in me. Why did it always end up being the wrong people? Fate could be downright perverse.

Zippo Comix was pretty jammed when I got there. I was surprised to see Mark at the door like he owned the place. If he asked me out, that would be the capper to my miserable week.

"Hey, Kari," he said. "I'm really glad you decided to come."

Come to what? What was going on? "I don't . . . I mean . . . sorry, come again?"

"To the signing. Glad you came. You're sort of a minor celebrity around here." He motioned at a large poster hanging just inside the doorway.

There in glorious blue, purple, and green was my comic book double in a leather superhero outfit that added dangerous curves the original clearly did not have. But the nose was there, big as life. Big, bold letters spelled out the name of the butt-kicking heroine: *Kari. A new comic by Jared Jameson, published by Mark Lennard Enterprises. Special signing from three to four o'-clock.* Once I got past the shock of it, I was flattered and peeved all at once. How dare Jared turn me into a caricature of myself? For a minute I forgot to feel guilty about not being in love with him.

I pushed my way to a table and picked up a debut copy of *Kari*. Leafing through, I saw that the story line had Kari kicking serious booty to defend her home planet. She lived in a castle with two mutts. The castle and the dogs looked hugely familiar. I hung around in the back, reading from cover to cover, till most of the people cleared out. Jared was packing up his pens and shaking out his autograph hand.

"Can you sign this?" I asked, extending my copy.

Jared stuck his hands in his jeans pockets and pulled his shoulders up to his ears. "I was gonna tell you about it."

"Along with other things?"

He stared off at a spot on the far wall above my head. "About that . . ."

Mark, oblivious to the bad timing, walked up. "Good signing, Jameson. I think we've got a hit on our hands. You must be proud to be the muse," he said, looking at me.

"Yeah, it's so great to be reduced to someone else's caricature."

"Kinda like making movies," Jared shot back.

Painfully good point.

"Well, congratulations," Mark said, walking off. He stopped. "Oh. And about that other matter?"

"555-1574," Jared said flatly. It was Dee's phone number. Mark wanted Dee's phone number? Once again I'd missed all the clues.

Jared was staring at me. I took another long look at my namesake. "She's really cool. I mean it, Jared. It's great. I wish I were like her."

"You are like her. You just don't know it."

Suddenly I felt like I could cry. "I really screwed everything up, didn't I?"

Jared smiled. "Yes. But you did it with style."

"Jared," I said, laughing through a fine mist of tears. "Remind me to hate you later."

"Sure. Kari?"

"Yeah?"

"Don't forget to hate me."

I stepped on his foot. He stepped on mine. I elbowed him in the ribs. He elbowed back harder. Before we could become the oldest people ever to play rock-paper-scissors, I made a suggestion.

"Wanna get out of here?"

"You bet."

We went for a long drive, ending up at the swimming hole, where we sat on the rocks. We talked about everything. I told him about Connor, the artist formerly known as Prince Charming, dumping me for Nan. He gave me the lowdown on his first comic book being published. All those covert conversations with Mark, I now realized, were about publishing his work. I was such a dork. Of course Mark recognized me from the comic book and wondered what was up with me, with us.

"I'm sorry about trying to fix you up with Dee," I said. "I really thought you had it for her."

"Malloy? She's a sweet girl. And a good bud. Okay, and I have to admit, I had some lustful thoughts here and there. But she's not right for me."

"She thinks you're a hottie," I said, giving the word all the girlish enthusiasm I knew Jared would hate. Old habits die hard.

"Kar, Dee would think Mr. Rogers was a hottie given the right mood. She's a little boy crazy."

I laughed.

Jared grinned his loopy grin and rested his chin on his knee. "So. You still haven't told me what you thought about . . . you know."

Here it came. We were getting along so nicely, I'd hoped we could just pretend it never happened. Just keep going like usual. "Well . . . I've been thinking, and . . ."

"That's okay," Jared said, standing up and throwing a stone at the pond. It sank. "You don't have to answer that."

I pulled him back down. "Yes. Yes, I do." How to begin? "The thing is, if I could fall in love with anybody, it would be you. I mean, we like the same things. We hate the same things. I witnessed your piercing. It's just . . . I don't feel . . . that way about you. I wish I did. You're my very best friend ever, and I love you. Maybe that's the problem. I'm sorry."

Jared stared down at the brightly colored comic version of me. He tore little bits of the cover into strips. "Yeah. I kinda figured that out. Well, the whole Connor experience did give me an inkling, but I thought it might be a good-looking-guy phase you were going through." His jaw clenched and unclenched, and I knew he was holding back hard.

"Do you hate me?" I asked, not really wanting an honest answer.

"Just a little," Jared said, sparing me nothing. "The truth is, if you and I dated, it would either be fireworks and grand opera, or it would be a total crash-and-burn fest where we'd spit whenever someone mentioned the other person's name." He rolled the comic book up like a newspaper two and three times. "I think I need to stay away from you for a while."

I felt sick. "How long is a while?"

"I'll let you know. If I haven't figured it out by the end of the summer, I'll just have to join the foreign legion. Meanwhile, can you give me a lift home? My car is officially dead and gone."

We opened all the windows and listened to the radio like we'd done a million times before, only it wasn't before, and we both knew it. He signed my comic book like it was a surreal yearbook. *Dear Kari, I didn't really get to know you. We had some classes together. Hope to see you kicking butt in the universe sometime. Have a good summer. Your friend, Jared.* Driving past my house, Jared gave a salute to Lila's Freak Castle.

"Man, you don't know how lucky you are, Karnage," he mused.

That anybody could call me lucky after my hideous

weekend floored me. "How do you figure that?" I asked.

"With a family like yours, you know you can be anything you want to be. No one cutting you down to size. Holding you back. Telling you how to be. It's a beautiful thing." His eyes twinkled for a minute, then he leaned halfway out the window. "People of Greenway! It's time to let your freak flag fly!" He screamed it again. People were staring. They stopped watering their manicured lawns and gawked. By the time we reached Jared's familiar mailbox, I was screaming, too.

"Freak flag! Fly your freaky deaky flags, folks!"

Jared and I laughed till we were hoarse. He shut the door and hovered for a minute, uncertain. "See you in September, Kari. By the way, I haven't forgotten that you owe me twenty bucks."

And he was gone. A rare bird in flight.

I stopped by Dee's house on the way home. She was lying on a towel in her backyard, getting a base for her summer tan. She couldn't believe Connor had gotten back together with Nan.

"Oh my God. Are you, like, hitting the Häagen Dazs yet? I would be."

"I'm too depressed for ice cream," I said with a sigh.

"I don't think I've ever been too bummed for Vanilla

Swiss Almond." She opened and closed a butterfly clip a zillion times. I reached out and took it away from her. "Sorry. Hey, Kari, I need to talk to you about something."

Oh no. Here it came. Pan over two friends talking. Tight shot of one friend, we'll call her Kari, proving what a royal creep she is by breaking other friend's heart. I rushed in. "Listen, I've been an A-1 turd of a friend lately. I'm sorry. I have a lot to learn. About everything."

Dee sat up fast. "It's okay. Just don't try to set me up with anybody again. I hope you're not mad, but I am so over Jared."

Mad? I wanted to hug her. I did. Then I started laughing hysterically in relief.

"What's so funny?"

"Everything." I sighed again.

"So listen." Dee's eyes were bright with excitement. "Jared's friend Mark is so babealicious. We really hit it off at your party. He called just before you showed up, and we talked for half an hour. He's taking me out next Friday. So, see, something good did come from your party." I smiled in spite of how I was feeling. Dee babbled on. "And do you know what his favorite movie is?"

"*Titanic*?" I offered meekly.

"No! *The Breakfast Club,* which is, like, my second-favorite movie of all time. Isn't that positively Roswell?"

Dee stretched back in the grass and reached her long, tapered fingers toward the sun, trying to pull it in with both hands.

"Totally," I said. And I meant it.

After dinner Mom and I sat outside with her tarot cards under the tattered tent Ever's Hardware made us buy. I had asked Mom for a reading. She chewed a fingernail and peered into my future, spread out on a card table. "These are wonderful cards, honey. Full of good things."

"Really? Like what?" I said, noticing the card that showed lightning striking a very large tower. Call me wacky, but it didn't seem to bode well.

Mom pointed to the tower card. "This is your recent past. Where you've been. Lots of . . . disruption." That was putting it mildly. "But it can also be like a storm that cleans everything away. And look, over here is the sun, promising light and confidence and happiness. Very good fortune. What's wrong?"

I had started crying. "I let everyone down. You. Lila. My friends." The last part came out as a whisper. "Daddy."

Mom led me by the hand. In the living room she pulled a dusty photo box from the middle of a pile of books and handed it to me. "Here," she said. "Take a look at this."

Inside were pictures that I'd never seen before. They were kind of screwy, frankly. Not all that artistic or well-ordered. I recognized Mom and Lila and the sproutlings, even though they were sometimes out of focus or cropped badly. But there was a freedom to the pictures. They made me feel happy. I kept wanting to look at them. "Who took these?" I asked.

"Your father," Mom answered, picking up a photo of Lila looking at me with a look of love on her face. He'd managed to catch her at just the right second. Before she turned sour again. "Your dad took these a few months before he died. They're my favorites. They're so . . . imperfect. He was learning, Kar."

I didn't understand. "Learning what?"

"To capture people's souls."

And then I knew what she meant. I had turned on my camera and tried to pull off a magic trick, not real magic. I hadn't seen into people's hearts. I hadn't even scratched the surface.

That night I took another look at my film school application. I scribbled the answer that came to mind. *I know how not to make a movie. The rest you'll have to teach me.*

chapter 14

The last week of school passed painfully slowly. Each day I walked down the halls of Greenway High, I was greeted by accusing stares and whispers behind my back. A few brave souls nodded in the halls and gave me the thumbs-up sign. One guy even asked me if his band could play my next party. I was either total bad news or a major rebel, depending on who was telling the story.

I saw Connor once in the commons. I was picking at my yogurt when he came over to sign my yearbook. *To Kari, a really cool chick. Remember me when you're famous. Love, Connor.* I had rated two lines and a signature. Still, it did say "love." After obsessing over whether that meant capital "love" or just "thanks for the memories," I finally decided to give it up and move on.

True to his word, Jared stayed out of sight, surfacing only for the last bell. As was our ritual, the two of us threw our papers up in the air, letting them drift down on the commons like out-of-season snow. But when I looked through the sheets of blankness, he was gone. I was really going to miss him.

When Lila got all her bats back from the animal control center, she was in the mood to celebrate. We piled into the Jesus mobile and made the long drive out to Tokyo Joe's. I figured Joe would be upset about all his plates and cups getting trashed at my party. But he was full of good cheer when we arrived. He seated us at a big table near the karaoke stage and brought us a pitcher full of Tumbleweed Tea, which was actually plain Lipton tea with a sprig of mint in each glass.

Joe offered Lila his hand like an old-fashioned cowboy. "Lila, I've got a new iguana, and he's a beaut. Want to have a look?"

Lila sprang out of her seat. "Would I! Tell me, what did you name him?"

Joe beamed with pride. "I'm calling him Iguana Go West." We all groaned in unison, which seemed to make Joe very happy.

"We need some action around here," Theo announced, heading for the stage. He plopped four quarters into the jukebox and watched as the lyrics to "The Streets of Laredo" scrolled up. Theo not only sang along, he acted out all the parts, down to the dying cowboy at the end. I have to admit, it was pretty funny. Isis sure thought so. At first she fought the smile tugging at her lips, but by the end of the song she was onstage with Theo, singing and playacting through a repertoire of country songs so old, even cable TV wouldn't run them in the dead of night.

Lila was stroking Iguana Go West, who seemed surprised to be so fawned over. I could swear he was purring, or whatever it is that reptiles do when they're feeling the love. Lila caught my eye for a second. I thought she was going to make me come over and pet Mr. Icky Green Thing. Instead she winked, reminding me of the grandma who smiled at me in a picture my dad took a hundred million years ago.

"Whatcha thinking?" Mom asked. She was chewing on a piece of raw ginger. The smell of it made my nose run.

"About Daddy," I answered truthfully. "I think . . . Promise you won't laugh?"

Mom smiled and kissed my cheek. "No."

I grabbed a California roll off her plate and peeled the seaweed off in layers. "I want to make a short movie. About Daddy." Mom's brows furrowed, and her smile widened. "About his passion for taking pictures. You know, like, the building of an artist. What do you think?"

"Hey, Mom!" Theo yelled. "Next we're gonna sing 'I Died in the Wool, but I Rose in the Garden,' okay?"

Mom gave a little wave as Theo and Isis prepared their next floor show. "I think," she said without looking

at me, "that strength should be your tarot card." It was a totally Mom answer, mysterious but somehow just right. And it would have to do.

Our waiter brought us barbecued tuna served up on plates shaped like saddles. "Two orders of Laguna Tuna. Can I get you anything else?" My head shot up, and I was face-to-face with some familiar brown, soulful eyes. I was staring like a love-starved freak. Which I pretty much was when you got down to it.

"Hey, Kari," our hottie of a waiter said sheepishly. It was John, the debater from my party.

"Hi," I said. "I didn't know you worked here." No duh.

John shrugged self-consciously. "My dad owns this place."

Now it made sense. John had come to my party to set up the food. I was glad to know that the crudité arranging in the kitchen wasn't an obsessive-compulsive thing because he really was cute.

Tokyo Joe came over and slapped an arm around his son. "Dobbins family, this is my son, John Wayne Hari, the fastest sushi server in the East. Just moved here from the West." Joe beamed with pride. John grimaced and practically hid behind his tray.

John Wayne Hari? It was too bad to be believed. Had I actually met a guy whose family was just as whacked

as mine? Open on establishing shot of hero and heroine commiserating over normal Tater Tots in neat silver Honda at Sonic drive-in. Cut. Take two. Open on hero and heroine in quirky Western sushi restaurant. He is mortified. She is . . . amused.

Not a bad opening. I'd have to see how the script developed. John refilled my tea. "So. What are you doing this summer?" he asked.

Signing a deal with Disney? Starting my own fashion line? Inventing a bubble gum that never loses its flavor? "Nothing much," I said. "How about you?"

"Working here," John said with a roll of his eyes. "By the way, I really thought your party was a good time."

"Thanks," I said. "That makes one."

"Seriously," John said, all wide-eyed. He didn't have anything else on the tray to give us, but he hung around, anyway. "So. Do you ever, like, hang out at that place everyone likes . . . Café Vortex?"

I thought about it for a minute. "No," I said.

"Me neither. Well, maybe I'll see you around this summer."

"Yeah. Maybe." I was starting to like this idea.

"Hey, pardner!" Tokyo Joe called to his son over Theo's awful warbling. "I think Miss Lila here needs a refill. Care to load up that pony express with something to wet the whistle?"

John sighed and leaned in close. "Please kill me."

I smiled, and he loped off into the sunset, or at least the smoke of the hibachi grill. On the way he turned and shook his head, sharing a private see-what-we-have-to-put-up-with moment. It made me want to doodle his name on my napkin. My summer started taking shape in my head. Something about John and me at the movies, holding hands, sharing freaky family stories.

John Wayne Hari. Hari and Kari. *Hari Kari?* It was just too perfect. I leaned back in my chair and let the laugh soar out of me like a balloon, bouncing high and free into the blue, blue sky.

About the Author

Libba Bray has written several plays, comedy sketches, and lots of advertising copy for products people absolutely do not need. Her most hellish memory of being sixteen was the time she had to wear a trash bag for a yearbook picture. (Don't ask.) A native Texan, she now lives in Brooklyn.